Lauren paced a n— ment. It might tal— going to keep walk— her system. It? Wh— ding? Him.

How could she have been so deceived? After all that had happened, hadn't she learned anything? She had believed in Flynn. She looked around her apartment. Memories of Flynn crowded at her. He had been wonderful to her after the robbery. He'd cleaned up the mess and stayed to make her feel safe. He'd kissed her. . . .

Carefully, he pulled the black ski mask down over his face. This was his last chance. And to think, they all thought Lauren's problems didn't have anything to do with him and Operation Blackford. Lucky for him! The only thing he hadn't gotten a good look at was her bedroom. He'd start there.

He swung the rope up and over, catching it so he could swing over to reach her bedroom. Noiselessly, he landed in the middle of the balcony. For a moment he stood listening, then he checked the street below. Reaching into his pocket, he drew out a long, slim knife.

BURIED SHADOWS

LESLIE LYNN

LYNX BOOKS
New York

BURIED SHADOWS

ISBN: 1-55802-100-0

First Printing/December 1988

This book is published by Lynx Books, a division of Lynx Communications, Inc., 41 Madison Avenue, New York, New York 10010. The name ''Lynx'' together with the logotype consisting of a stylized head of a lynx is a trademark of Lynx Communications, Inc.

Printed in the United States of America

0 9 8 7 6 5 4 3 2 1

To the J.R.s in our lives

BURIED SHADOWS

PROLOGUE

"I know what you've been up to." Dr. Bernard Jamieson curled his fingers even more tightly around the telephone receiver to control their trembling. "Why you of all people should resort to this . . ." he continued, his voice weakening, overpowered by the relentless voice on the other end of the receiver. Tears slipped unheeded down Bernard's ruddy cheeks as he listened.

Drawing a deep breath, he spoke again, this time more sharply. "I'm sorry, too. But that can't be helped now. I've documented everything." His hand lay flat over a single yellow legal sheet covered with dates, and with effort he again stilled his trembling fingers. "I'll be contacting the authorities first thing in the morning." Shaking his head, his shoulders slumped as if weighed down by unbelievable weariness. "No . . . No . . . This is beyond me, beyond family. I'm sorry, dear boy, but you brought this upon yourself."

His eyes, blank with sorrow, searched the familiar room for solace. The priceless pottery, so dear to him, offered no answers. His well-read tomes on Egyptology and antiquities, textbooks and treatises on archaeology and ancient pottery; these books which lined every shelf gave no comfort. The paintings, lovingly collected over fifty years, held no escape. His eyes rested on the antique dueling épées crossed over the fireplace. They were a symbol: Honor, after all, was the key, and personal honor above all else. Family and friends, right or wrong, could be defended, but personal integrity required the keenest defense.

The voice on the other end of the phone line stopped pleading and became harsh with demands. Bernard stooped over, his head nearly touching against the open volume of *The Pictorial History of Etruscan Ceramics* until his body seemed to curl up into itself.

Suddenly, the receiver fell to the desk, then landed on the carpet, its disembodied voice still sputtering angrily. Clutching at his heart, Bernard struggled for breath. Fumbling for the ever-present pill bottle in his sweater pocket, he pried off the cap and quickly put one tiny pill under his tongue. Relief was slow in coming: so slow, so slight the lessening of the tightness in his chest that he knew all too well.

Honor, above all, must be preserved.

A vise was slowly squeezing the breath from his body, but he found the strength to lift a pencil and scribble hieroglyphics in the margin of the book. This copy was for Lauren. He took the single yellow paper from his desk and folded it in half again and again, until it was less than an inch wide. Pushing himself up from the desk, he stumbled to the far bookcase and the book he needed. Carefully and with some effort he took it down from the shelf, bent back the binding, and slipped the folded sheet into the small gap. Sagging weakly against the shelves, he turned the book over and over in his hands, assuring himself that the evidence he'd compiled was completely hidden. Only then did he gently slip the book back into place, where it fit perfectly beside its companion volumes.

Satisfied, his strength finally gave out and he sank to his knees. Half crawling, half dragging himself, he managed to reach the overstuffed reading chair. His eyes focused on the table beside it and the object he wished to hold one last time. Leveraging himself up, he felt for the large silver-framed picture of a woman with coiled gray hair and serene eyes. "Martha . . ." he whispered his deceased wife's name, sinking slowly back against the chair.

The old man had said on the phone that he'd made a list. It had to be here somewhere.

All the shocked relatives had been here

to peek and pry, to wonder, but finally the ambulance had taken the body away. Not until this moment had he had the opportunity to look around. He was sorry for the old man, too, but there was a job to be done.

The logical place to start was here in the study. Methodically, he went through the desk examining every scrap of paper and then putting it carefully back into place. Nothing.

He wasn't going to give himself away now. Not after all these months of hard work to find the right people—the people who were willing to pay the right price. Finished at the desk, he moved to the first bookcase. If it took all night he would find the damned thing. Carefully, he shook out every book.

Maybe it was better this way. Now he wouldn't have to worry. It had been a mistake to involve the old man. He couldn't believe Dr. Jamieson had discovered the truth; what would have made him suspicious?

Slowly, he searched every shelf, looked into vases and wooden trinket boxes, pulled pictures off the walls. He checked every imaginable hiding place. Still nothing. Going back to the desk, he sat down and tried to imagine Dr. Jamieson sitting there talking on the phone. The heart attack had happened right here. What had the old man done with the list?

The book that lay open on the desk was a surprise; the old man hadn't been into ceramics for years. The last time he'd really taken the time to make pleasant small talk with the Dr. Jamieson, he'd been full of stories about a young woman he'd met at the museum—he was going senile, or at least, that's what he'd thought until he'd been discovered by him. He slammed one fist down on the desk. No one was going to get the better of him now!

At least he was safe for the moment. He'd be back again to search the other rooms. The bedroom next. Poor old fool, he thought to himself, going on and on about the family honor. Might made right. Pretty soon they'd all understand their mistakes—ignoring him, passing him over. He remembered them all.

His eyes searched the room again. There on the table next to Dr. Jamieson's favorite easy chair was a framed picture of his beloved wife which had been removed from the dead man's hands. That was it! Chortling, he sprang across the room and cautiously pried the picture apart.

"Damn!" he cursed in fury when the frame revealed nothing but a dusty oval of cardboard.

Well, he had the perfect excuse to be in and out of the place whenever he liked. After all, he'd been a favorite. He'd just have to go over everything again and again un-

til he found it. Then nothing could touch him.

Up until this point, everything had gone exactly according to schedule. He'd see it stayed that way.

1 Lauren was late. The one badly bent spoke of her umbrella sent a steady stream of rain halfway down her back. If she could just turn the umbrella to the right ... Her purse flipped from under her arm and fell to the wet sidewalk.

"Oh, hell!"

Before she could bend to pick it up, a long, navy-clad arm came into her line of vision and scooped the purse off the pavement. "Here you are," a man's voice said.

The umbrella blocked her view. Tilting it back she started, "Thank ..." but the tall stranger had turned his back to talk to a policeman standing stoically in the sudden spring downpour. In an effort to get the man's attention, Lauren finished loudly, "... you." But it was to no avail, for the policeman had pointed down the street toward approaching sirens, and both men were caught up in the motorcade's arrival.

Dismissing him with a shrug of her shoulders, she raced up the steps and closed her umbrella, placing it in the stand next to the door. Breathless from her five-block run from the bus stop, she crossed the narthex. The scent of flowers—dozens of roses, gladiolas, carnations, and mums—hung heavily in the oak-paneled University of Chicago chapel.

Two men turned to watch her enter. Both looked nervous and tense, as if they would rather be anywhere than this hushed, sweet-scented entryway, but while the tall blond smiled politely, a scowl darkened the shorter one's face.

"Hello." Her voice came out in a cracked whisper. "I'm Lauren Michaels."

The blond man, attractively tanned for so early in the spring, took her outstretched hand between his wide palms. His azure eyes lit with appreciation. "Lauren, I'm Chuck Jamieson. Uncle Bernard spoke of you so often, I feel I know you." He looked to the shorter, stockier man who waited patiently at his side. "Malcolm, this is Uncle Bernard's Lauren from the Field Museum."

Malcolm nodded, his small, close-set dark eyes appraising her solemnly behind thick glasses. "Of course. Uncle Bernard was quite fond of you. Malcolm Carlson. How do you do, Miss Michaels?"

Lauren's gaze slipped over Chuck, so exactly like his great-uncle had described him: a bit over average height, blond hair that curled in spite of expensive styling, impeccably tailored three-piece gray suit with a crisp white shirt, a striped burgundy tie, and monogrammed cuff links. Her gaze then settled on Malcolm, strangely tense and completely unlike the picture Bernard had portrayed of the family peacemaker. His navy pinstripe suit was calculated to lend him height, yet the effect was defeated by a light blue, white-collared shirt and a paisley tie. How Dr. Jamieson had loved these two, the sons he never had.

"I'm sorry about Dr. Jamieson." The small, hard lump of pain squeezed into her throat once again, as it had so often these past ten days.

"Thank you. It was very sudden. His heart . . ."

"Chuck," Malcolm interrupted. "They're about to begin the memorial service. There are some seats available toward the back, Miss Michaels. Thank you for coming." Malcolm even managed a slight curving of his lips, which was meant, no doubt, to be a smile, but by then Lauren had been dismissed. Chuck had gently squeezed her fingers before she turned away to find one of the last empty chairs.

The chapel was filled with men and women whose lives had been touched by Dr. Jamieson, just as her own had been. She found it hard to believe it was only eighteen months ago that she had first spied him at the Field Museum, sitting on a wooden bench surrounded by display cases of sixth century sarcophagi, looking, even in this unlikely setting, exactly like her childhood vision of Santa Claus. After her toil among the shards and wraps of the Egyptian collection, she felt as if Isis had led her to this extraordinary man: curly white hair, ruddy cheeks, and bright eyes that sparkled with life, incongruous among the Etruscan antiquities. She had wanted to talk to him, to find out if he was as kindly and knowledgeable as he seemed. Yet she hadn't intruded, for he had been absorbed in conversation with another scholar.

However, on his next visit he was alone and, astonishingly, was reading a hardbound book that was one of her favorite novels: *Pawn in Frankincense* by Dorothy Dunnett. If this man was her long-forsaken dream-vision of Santa, the hero of Dunnett's books, Lymond, was her romantic fantasy.

Dr. Jamieson had glanced up, and he had fairly caught her staring. One white bushy brow rose over his gleaming green eyes. "Excellent book. You should read it," he advised, a smile splitting his pristine moustache and beard.

"I have," she said with a laugh. "All six books in the series at least five times each. I've a mad passion for Lymond."

Widening his eyes, which seemed to hold laughter, he gently teased, "Ah, at last. A young woman of exceptional taste. Haven't I seen you here at the museum before?"

"I work here, in the Egyptian collection. I'm the assistant curator."

"Ah, so you're responsible for these excellent new displays. I've been coming here for years, but in the last few months I've noticed some impressive innovations."

Lauren shook her head. "They're not all my doing. Bea Simpson is the curator, and we work on them together. She has some wonderful ideas. I'll pass your compliment on to her."

"Please do." He patted the bench beside him. "Sit down, my dear, if you have a moment."

Those moments had added up week after week, growing more frequent and eagerly anticipated, until Lauren realized with wonder and happiness that Dr. Jamieson enjoyed her companionship as much as she did his. Until she met him, she hadn't realized just how lonely she was. He had shared so much with her; golden tales of his decades as a professor of ancient history at the University of Chicago, and of his travels around the world. His mind was a vast storehouse of knowledge and insight which he generously laid open to her questioning.

Remembering their unceasing arguments about a possible link between the Etruscan and Egyptian ceramics, Lauren's mouth curved into a small smile. He encouraged her hidden ambition to teach hands-on workshops demonstrating the intricate designs of ancient pottery: "You're right, Lauren. Looking at antiquity behind a glass case may be awe-inspiring to some, but it's awfully dry. Now if you can actually touch . . . and perhaps create, then you have gone beyond teaching to experiencing."

And he had taught her every Tuesday and Friday afternoon for six months, sitting on "his" bench surrounded by priceless Etruscan treasures. Memories of those coffee breaks, she so timid at first, and their weekly lunches, made her ache a little with loneliness. He had become her family. Family—now she had lost hers for the second time.

How could he be suddenly gone forever? The burning in her eyes made her blink several times as she struggled not to cry and stared down at her tightly laced fingers. When she felt someone slide into the vacant seat beside her, she shifted slightly in her chair. A quartet of musicians from the Chicago Symphony had been playing a soft piece by Mozart, and now, a soprano Lauren recognized from the Lyric Opera Company walked to the front of the chapel.

"Ave Maria." The powerful aria flowed around her, and as the last pure note of the soprano's voice faded, Lauren's struggle ended and a tear fell on the back of her folded hands. Another followed it, and she opened her bag, frantically searching for a Kleenex, anything to catch the tears brimming beneath her lashes. From beside her, a navy-clad arm reached out and a long-fingered hand offered a folded white handkerchief. She took it, pressing it to each eye before turning, and without looking up, nodded carefully to acknowledge her second rescue. The chaplain rose to make his comments and Lauren took a deep, steadying breath, refolding the square of cotton before again blotting her eyes. Determinedly, she put aside her self-pity to listen with interest to the minister's recollections of her extraordinary friend. She had always thought that Dr. Jamieson was as lonely as she, but now she learned he had numerous colleagues, friends, and interests. She was fortunate that he had counted her among them, especially as it became evident that he had some influence—money, and power in high places. The mayor and half the city council were in attendance. He rated a police honor guard. Still, he had taken the time to befriend her.

Absorbed with her discoveries of a side of Dr. Jamieson's life she hadn't known existed, she was unaware that the rustle of movement around her signaled the end of the service until a low murmur sounded above her. "I'll miss Dr. Jamieson, too. He was very special."

At last, Lauren looked up at the owner of the handkerchief. It was indeed her rescuer from outside. The thick salt-and-pepper hair was deceiving, for his face was young and lean, with tired lines showing around exceptionally piercing blue eyes now filled with sadness. He had a wide, generous mouth and an exceptionally strong jaw, which he now stroked as he stood absolutely still, absorbing her gaze without discomfort. She knew she was staring, and thrust her hand forward to introduce herself.

"Flynn, I didn't see you arrive," Chuck broke in, bringing both of them to their feet, and Lauren's hand fell to her side. "Oh, you've met Uncle Bernard's Lauren."

"You're ... Lauren?" The stranger's eyes were now lit by his smile, and its fervor surprised her. "You were Dr. Jamieson's favorite topic of conversation."

Warmth spread to her cheeks, and she looked questioningly at both men, then allowed her gaze to linger on the unknown Flynn. "Yes, I'm Lauren Michaels. How do you do?"

"Flynn Fitzgerald. It's good to meet you at last, Miss Michaels."

This was Fitzgerald ... the man Dr. Jamieson had described to her on so many occasions, always beaming with approval at the mention of his name. A romantic hero like Lymond, handsome and charming, he'd said. He had wanted them to meet, but she had discouraged it as gently as she could, not wanting to hurt the doctor's feelings. She had thrilled to his descriptions of Flynn, a maverick, but nonetheless a man of sensitivity and charm. Clearly, Dr. Jamieson had felt they would like each other.

Lauren, however, hadn't been ready to trust anyone else yet. But maybe Dr. Jamieson had been right. Even here, with her thoughts weighed with sadness, Lauren felt the tug of Flynn's charm as she openly stared at him, his long, mobile mouth curving appealingly.

"Flynn's an old friend." Chuck's voice cut into her thoughts. "Malcolm and I both work for him in the U.S. Attorney's office."

Confused by Flynn's admiring gaze, she turned gratefully from those intense blue eyes to smile at Chuck.

"Your uncle often spoke of your investigations for the Criminal Division. He was very proud of your work. I know you made him feel a part of your success."

A strange redness appeared in Chuck's face, as if he were embarrassed by the compliment, and this surprised her. "He played a big part in our success—Malcolm's and mine. He helped put us both through law school, you know. He was even responsible for our meeting Flynn," he said, turning toward Flynn. "Remember?"

Nodding, Flynn's mouth turned up at the corners. "How could I forget? It was the first day. We were all moving into our apartments near Northwestern. We met at the grocery store. I'd forgotten my wallet. . . ."

"And your checkbook," Chuck added with a laugh.

"Yeah, and the store wasn't about to offer credit to a first-year law student. But Bernard did."

"And invited you back with us to his house for one of Aunt Martha's great dinners," Chuck added with a smile.

Lauren's chest tightened as she watched the men reminisce, their faces illuminated with remembered happiness and shared warmth. Dr. Jamieson had had that effect on people. He brought out their capacity for joy. He had done that for her, too, even though she'd thought that capacity to be deeply buried in the shadows of her past.

"And you've all been friends ever since," she interjected quietly.

"Not just friends. Chuck and Malcolm are my two right arms." Flynn gripped Chuck's shoulder. "I'd trust them with my life. But right now, Chuck, I think Malcolm is signaling to you. He's with that lady in the red flowered hat."

"Oh, my god, it's Great-Aunt Matilda. Poor Malcolm," Chuck responded with an exaggerated grimace. "Thanks for coming, Lauren. I hope I see you again sometime."

Flustered now that she was alone with Flynn, Lauren refolded his handkerchief. "Thank you . . ." She hesitated. "I'll launder this and return it to you as soon as possible."

"Nonsense," he retorted abruptly and a great deal too loudly. Flushing, Lauren averted her eyes from his face as the press of the crowd surrounding her forced her to start toward the exit. As she reached the door, she turned back to find Flynn close behind her and studying her with peculiar intensity. Just at that moment, they broke into the bright sunlight. The storm was over. Flynn took her arm possessively.

Lauren stiffened in response, and she knew he felt it, for he dropped his hand and tilted his head to meet her eyes. "Come have coffee with me." It was a statement, not a question, and for the first time she heard the faintest echo of an Irish lilt. "Bernard would be pleased that we've finally met. I'd like to have someone to share those good memories of him with."

He was smiling now, charm turned on full, looking exactly like Dr. Jamieson's description of him as the answer to every girl's prayer. Lauren immediately squelched the little flicker of warmth that burst to life at that smile. She should make an excuse and walk away, but she knew he was speaking the truth; Dr. Jamieson would indeed be pleased by their meeting. Giving in to her need to hold onto Dr. Jamieson a while longer, she nodded.

The French Baker was a cheerful little restaurant with blue checkered tablecloths and fancy priscilla curtains. Flynn ordered hot almond croissants and, at Lauren's suggestion, spiced tea.

He took the tray with the teapot and led her to a table near the back of the roc

She could sense him studying her, and it was puzzling. Perhaps the feeling was not so surprising, however. She'd been feeling unsettled for a long time, but particuliarly so since Dr. Jamieson's death.

The night Dr. Jamieson had first invited her to his home for dinner and to examine some rare books, Lauren had let down her guard for the first time in a long while.

A beautiful centerpiece of wild roses and ivy from the garden had adorned the cherrywood dining room table. It was set with Waterford crystal, blue and white Wedgewood china, and shining silver. Although she had wanted to help, he had insisted everything was under control. She slid into the chair he pulled out for her and waited until he came back through the swinging kitchen doors. It was then that she had burst into tears, for he'd been carrying a silver chafing dish exactly like one of her mother's that they'd had to sell. And it held a chicken tetrazzini, her favorite dish.

She hadn't realized how badly she had needed to talk until Dr. Jamieson, with compassion and understanding, gently drew it all out of her that night. That had been the beginning of the healing process. From that night on, she felt she was slowly regaining control of her life and learning to be happy.

Wasn't that why she had decided to come with Flynn? Dr. Jamieson had always wanted them to meet, and it seemed the least she could do.

Their discussion focused at first on generalities, and they appeared to have much in common. Both were only children with parents no longer living, and each devoted long hours to their work. Although Flynn had many friends, she sensed he was somewhat of a loner. Flynn seemed to be all Dr. Jamieson had said, yet there was something about him that disturbed her. One moment he was perfectly charming, and the next moment all his perfection seemed too overwhelming, almost like a performer reciting exactly the right words. Yes, that was it—Flynn was too perfect.

"Dr. Jamieson talked of you so much, I feel I know you, Lauren. Do you feel that about me, too?" he asked quietly, staring at her as if he found it difficult to believe she was sitting here with him.

"I think I know more about your work than I do about you," she replied, her fingers nervously circling the rim of the teacup. From all he had told her, Flynn rarely socialized or dated, yet she found it difficult to accept the fact that a man so charming and good-looking, with a prestigious job as well, could lead so quiet a life.

The blue eyes flamed, suddenly fierce. "My work? What an unusual topic for you to discuss."

"Well, we really spent most of our time discussing archaelogy or arguing about pottery. He had some unusual theories linking Etruscan and Egyptian cultures through their artisans. We spent hours debating, and it took days of research in the library to keep up with him." Hesitating at Flynn's fixed smile, she realized she was probably boring him and finished quietly, "I found him a great challenge intellectually."

"Yes, he was a smart man. Too smart to be taken in for long. . . ."

"Taken in?" she interrupted. His words and the growing tension of his body made her wonder if he was talking about her and her friendship with Dr. Jamieson. "What do you mean?"

He looked apologetic—the slow, appealing curve of his lips and the warmth in his ice-blue eyes. "Lauren, what I meant—" He was cut off by their number being called. The croissants were ready.

"Excuse me. I'll be right back." Flynn rose to get their order. He was so polite. . . .

The other lawyer had been polite, too, Lauren remembered. "I'm so sorry you have to be involved in all of this—"His earnest dark eyes and gentle manner had convinced her of his genuine compassion. "I'll help you and your mother, Lauren. Just tell me everything you know about your stepfather's dealings."

She had been incredibly naive. She'd told him everything she could remember: names of people she'd delivered packages to for her stepfather, dates, places. She remembered him writing everything down, encouraging her when she faltered, being unbelievably patient.

Then at the trial he'd turned on her.

"Surely, Miss Michaels, you suspected something."

No one had defended her. Technically, *she* wasn't on trial; and spreading the blame had served the best interests of her stepfather's lawyer as well.

"No . . . no, you know . . ."

"Just answer the question. You never guessed you were receiving money?"

"No, I . . ."

"Where, Miss Michaels, did you think the new car, your college education, the fancy clothes, and the big house were coming from?"

"My mother said my stepfather had gotten a promotion."

"Did you ever see him at work?"

"Well, yes. He asked me to do him some favors."

"And you agreed, not knowing those favors included delivering illegal stock tips? Come, come, Miss Michaels, don't expect this jury to believe you know nothing."

"But I . . ."

"And at the end, when your stepfather started embezzling to keep you in your high-class life-style, you expect us to believe you knew nothing of that, either?"

She'd felt stripped bare in that courtroom. He'd made it sound as if her stepfather had to resort to illegal means to support her.

"I had a trust fund from my natural father to pay for my education. I didn't ask him"—she gestured across the courtroom toward her stepfather—"for anything."

"And there was nothing ... else ... between you and your stepfather?"

His innuendo had horrified her.

There had been a startled gasp from the crowd that was packed into the small courtroom. She watched her mother half rise from her seat and then, mercifully, slide into a faint. Over the clamor, Lauren answered clearly, concisely, staring back at the attorney as if her life depended on it, "Absolutely not!" Rising to her feet, she turned frantically to the judge. "Please, your honor, I must go to my mother!" She had fought her way to her mother's side.

It wasn't until later that she realized why the prosecutor had acted in such a manner—the more sensational the trial, the more valuable the verdict would be. Now a full partner in the most prestigious law firm in Muncie, Indiana, the lawyer had gotten exactly what he wanted: a conviction, but of even more importance—fame.

And she had lost everything. First her friends and her home, and then a year later, with her mother's death, she lost her only family.

Flynn returned with the tray of croissants, startling her out of her uneasy reverie. Again he looked genuinely concerned. Did they teach them how to do this in law school—how to put you at ease until they were ready to pounce?

"Did I say something to upset you, Lauren? I didn't mean to. I was thinking of a recent case. Hard to believe that an intelligent man could be so consistently deceived. Bernard would never have let that happen to him."

"No, he wouldn't," she agreed. She had no idea what Flynn was talking about, but she was eager to concentrate on something besides her memories. "Dr. Jamieson was amazingly astute. I once had a problem with a co-worker and he knew immediately how to deal with it."

"I know what you mean. He had this logical mind that required you to lay everything out step by step. Sometimes it meant I completely reorganized a case after I talked to him. One time I even discovered I suspected the wrong man."

"The Fairchild case." Flynn's head snapped up from the tea he was pouring, and Lauren explained herself. "Dr. Jamieson said you were tilting at windmills with that one. He painted you as a real romantic hero."

She flushed at the intensity of his gaze. Dr. Jamieson's term for him had just popped out. Hero, especially romantic hero, was not a phrase she should have used at this stage in their relationship. What a strange thought. There was no relationship. A friendship, just beginning, perhaps . . . except it didn't feel right to her, despite Dr. Jamieson's predictions.

"I'm sorry." She smiled apologetically. "What were you saying?"

"I just wondered what else Bernard said about me or my cases?" His look was encouraging, but his eyes were strangely blank.

"He never got too specific about anything except that Fairchild case," she said carefully, as if she were on the witness stand again. Maybe all lawyers talked like this. "I think he honestly felt he deserved full credit for that one. And, of course, he followed your career closely, what with his nephews working in your office."

She hesitated, sorrow again tightening in her throat. "You know, I felt that maybe something was bothering him this last month. I wish I'd known about his heart condition. Maybe he felt the last attack was near." Her troubled eyes studied Flynn's set face. "Maybe I could have done something to help him."

His blue eyes warmed. "I know you helped him just by being his friend," Flynn said soothingly, and for the first time Lauren really wanted to believe him. "Bernard was very lonely after Martha's death. He said you reminded him of her." He studied her face carefully, and as his eyes narrowed into slits, she straightened unconsciously in her chair. "He was right."

There it was again, the strange intensity which could suddenly appear in Flynn's expression no matter where he was or what he was doing.

"I should have met you before. But this case I'm on has been giving me a lot of trouble, and I haven't had time for anything else," he continued.

"Operation Blackford," she answered quietly, sitting back in her chair, away from him.

He leaned over the table, his motion jeopardizing the teapot. When she reached to move it out of his way, he grasped her hand tightly. "What do you know about that?"

Startled, she stared at him, her hand aching a little from the strong grip of his fingers. "Mostly what I've read in the papers. But Dr. Jamieson told me Chuck and Malcolm were working very closely with you on it. He seemed puzzled at the trouble you've been having getting convictions." The hand holding hers tightened slightly, and she looked at it pointedly, then back at his face.

"I'm sorry," he offered almost absently, releasing her hand. "I think we should be going. I'll be happy to drop you at home."

"Thanks, but I'm going back to the museum. I really appreciate everything: the tea, the handkerchief . . ." She floundered, flustered as he stood watching her. "Well, again, it was nice to meet you, Flynn. How should I get the clean handkerchief back to you?"

Flynn's mouth curled into a tight smile. "Don't worry, Lauren. We'll be seeing more of each other."

Flynn Fitzgerald tilted his swivel chair back as far as it would go and stretched his weary arms out over his head. Why did he want to see her again, especially if somehow she was connected to the whole case? It couldn't be, not really. There was no way she could have gotten that kind of information, he told himself. Unless Chuck or Malcolm had inadvertently told their uncle, and she had wormed it out of him. . . .

But if Lauren Michaels was all Dr. Jamieson had said she was, that would never have happened. And indeed, she seemed to be the ideal woman Bernard had raved about. But Dr. Jamieson hadn't described that long and touseled honey-blond hair . . . those sexy cat's eyes . . . the full, sensuous lower lip . . . the sleek grace of her lithe body. Lauren was a beauty. But Dr. Jamieson had only talked of her intelligence and her compassion, her warmth and kindness to a lonely old man.

It just didn't make sense. None of it did.

Flynn turned his back on his desk and stared out the window at Lake Michigan. He did his best thinking while watching the sailboats tilt against the wind on the lake, a skill that seemed effortless from his vantage point. Only an experienced sailor knew the forces pulling between the sails and the rudder. Whenever his own work overwhelmed him or decisions seemed too difficult, Flynn would spread his fingers against his desk, push the swivel chair around, and watch the boats plow through the foam. Forces . . . everywhere.

As he concentrated on a Hobie-16 trying to come about, the phone rang. "Taggart, hello!" His chair snapped to attention. "Thanks for getting back to me so soon. I've got a job for you." Flynn raked his long fingers through his graying hair. "I want you to follow a woman. Very discreetly."

He turned back to look at the lake. It was empty, all the sailboats out of his line of sight.

"Her name? Lauren Michaels. You'll find her at the Field Museum."

2 Lauren was working in the dimly lit storeroom of the Field Museum, shoving the crate of Etruscan swords out of the way, when Beatrice appeared in the doorway. "Phone call for you, Lauren."

Swinging around, she hit her shin on the edge of the crate. "Damn!" Rubbing her leg, she limped away from the shelves lining the wall where she had been working and to a chair. "When are they going to open this crate and get it out of here!"

"The weapons exhibit goes up in three weeks," Beatrice soothed in her best "curator of the Egyptian collection" voice. "You have a phone call."

"Tell them to call back." Lifting her throbbing leg out of her black pump, she rubbed it gently. "I've got to inventory the new pots."

Beatrice lowered her gray-haired head slightly to peer over half-glasses. "It's a man, dear."

Slipping her foot back into her shoe, Lauren stood. "Which line?"

"Two-oh-four."

Lauren limped down the short hallway. Maybe it was Flynn. She had been thinking about him all week, wondering if he would follow up on his cryptic reference to future meetings. She told herself she didn't want him to call, that getting involved with a lawyer was the last thing she wanted. But the image of Flynn as a romantic hero persisted. It must be him on the phone. She hadn't gotten a call from a member of the opposite sex since she'd come to Chicago, which had been just fine with her. Until now.

Fortunately, she wouldn't have to negotiate three flights of stairs to her usual office. It was being painted, so she had the use of a phone and desk in a tiny cubbyhole in the basement, near the collection. Her pulse racing, she took a deep breath before picking up the phone and punching in the right line. "Lauren Michaels."

"Lauren, this is Malcolm Carlson."

"Oh, hello, Malcolm." She sagged onto the edge of her desk, trying to hide her disappointment. "This is a surprise. How are you?"

"Fine, thanks." He cleared his voice, and Lauren could almost see him jabbing nervously at his glasses, a mannerism of his she had noticed at the memorial service.

"Uncle Bernard has requested that certain books in his library be given to you.

Chuck and I have been down here at the house every day sorting things out. When could you stop by?"

"That was very nice of him." Lauren swallowed hard, emotional at the thought of a bequest from Dr. Jamieson. "I can come this afternoon." Glancing at her watch, she assigned the Egyptian pots to another day. "I could take the culture bus and be there in forty-five minutes."

"Fine. I'll see you then."

Beatrice appeared before the receiver could settle into its cradle and propped herself against the doorframe. She studied Lauren's face intently and then said quietly, "Well, obviously it wasn't *him*."

"What do you mean, *him*?" Lauren frowned and moved around the desk to her chair, forgetting the pain in her leg.

"Him. The man you've been mooning over all week. Well, not precisely mooning," Bea laughed. "Just jumping every time the phone rings."

"That is totally ridiculous, Bea. I have never *mooned* around about a man in all of my twenty-eight years, and I'm certainly not going to begin now. Although . . ." She couldn't prevent a wry smile from curving her mouth, and she finished dramatically, "He is one of the most gorgeous men I've ever met in my whole life."

Bea's face beamed, an expression Lauren associated more with her triumphant forays into archives than discussions about men. "At last! Tell me everything."

"Everything? There's hardly anything to tell," Lauren stalled, knowing full well that Beatrice would much rather drag it out of her than quickly be told the mundane truth: She had met Flynn Fitzgerald, at last, and despite her professed indifference to all men, he refused to fade from her thoughts for reasons that she didn't fully understand, while she had obviously been totally forgettable.

"What does he look like?" demanded Beatrice.

"Tallish. Wonderful, thick, salt-and-pepper hair. Broad shoulders. Incredible blue eyes," she teased vaguely, knowing Bea loved it. Silently, she thanked Dr. Jamieson for restoring to her the gift of humor. Letting her gaze drift about the ceiling, she smiled. "Handsome doesn't precisely fit. Perfection? Maybe."

"What's his name? Where did you meet him?" Beatrice quizzed, exasperation pursing her lips. She had been working with Lauren for over a year, and although they had a good relationship, Lauren had never been able to talk to her about anything personal. It was as if Lauren didn't have a social life. Bea, in her sixties, and despite gray hair, bifocals, and academic life, dated a number of men. Lauren, young and beautiful, seemed to lead the life of the cloister. Beatrice settled into the only extra chair in the cramped room, prepared to drag every detail out of her if need be.

"His name is Flynn Fitzgerald. He's an old friend of Dr. Jamieson's. I met him at the memorial service."

"How old is he?"

Lauren shrugged. "I don't know."

Bea frowned. "He's not a contemporary of Dr. Jamieson's or . . . or . . . mine, is he?"

Lauren leaned forward over the desk, resting her chin on the heel of her hand, and asked brightly, "Well, I don't know, Bea. Just how old are you?"

"Don't sass your superior, young lady. You might lose this incredibly well-paid position. Besides, you know I never discuss age or weight." Laughing, she gave a self-conscious tug on her blouse, smoothing it over her hips. Beatrice was not overweight, but having been rail-thin for most of her life, she despaired over the more shapely curves middle age had brought. Bea, however, was not one to complain, to others or to herself, about life's little struggles. Perhaps that was why Lauren admired her so much. Beatrice's cheerful optimism was a welcome break from her own brooding.

Relenting, Lauren smiled. "I guess he's in his mid-thirties. He has the look of a man who has been around."

"Around where? What's he do?"

"He's the Chief of the Criminal Division for the office of the U.S. Attorney."

"That's good." Beatrice nodded sagely. "Attorneys make good husbands."

"Husbands!" She looked at her friend in shock. "Beatrice, I don't even know the man. I've only spent an hour in his company." She couldn't let Bea, however unwittingly, add to the confusing pictures running through her head. "No. He's obviously not interested, or he would have called. And that's that."

She wasn't aware she had voiced that last thought until Beatrice reassured her, "Now, honey, the man might be busy or out of town. Trust me, he'll call."

Lauren thought of the handkerchief, cleaned, pressed, and carefully packaged in tissue paper. While she was ironing it she had discovered the initials *E.F.F.* finely hand-embroidered in one corner. What did the *E* stand for? Dr. Jamieson had never called him anything but Flynn Fitzgerald when he had spoken of him, which had been often. There had been a definite twinkle in his eyes as he plotted a meeting between the two of them. She'd hated disappointing Dr. Jamieson, but she had constantly made excuses for herself, and even for Flynn, pointing out that he was a very busy man.

It was her fault that she couldn't let go of the past. Since moving to Chicago, she just hadn't found her feet. Perhaps that was why she felt vaguely uneasy about Flynn. Maybe if she could meet him again she would feel differently; and Flynn had said they would meet again. But when?

She glanced at her watch and sprang up, glad for an excuse to escape Bea's watchful eyes. "Oh goodness, I've got to catch the three-forty-five to Hyde Park. It's never on schedule. I've got to run."

"Hyde Park? Why?"

"No time, Bea. I promise I'll tell all tomorrow. Bye."

Lauren was glad she'd run the last block because the bus miraculously pulled up five minutes early. Half an hour later, it dropped her near Dr. Jamieson's house, an oasis in the slow decay of a once-affluent section of Chicago. His great-nephews, concerned over his safety, had wanted him to move to a smaller apartment that would also be less trouble for him, but he'd refused, saying he needed the space for his books and papers. His home had been the carriage house of a large mansion that was now gone, and it was completely surrounded by a high brick wall. Inside that wall he had preserved Martha's perfect English garden, where he and Lauren had enjoyed many an afternoon tea.

Lauren rang the bell beside the wrought iron gateway, which clicked open automatically as Malcolm emerged from the front door. "Thank you for coming so promptly. Please go into the library. I've stacked the books my uncle selected for you there."

It seemed odd to see sheets thrown over

the upholstered furniture, and no fresh flowers from the garden on the dining room table. Everywhere neat stacks of the contents of drawers and cupboards covered the shining wood surfaces. Dr. Jamieson had a story about every piece of furniture and *objet d'art* that he and Martha had collected from around the world. His stories had peopled Lauren's lonely world, and once he saw that she really enjoyed listening, he'd shared so much with her. Those memories kept the older, darker ones at bay, and she cherished them.

When Malcolm joined her in the library, she turned to him. "I feel strange accepting these books. Are you sure you or some other member of your family doesn't want them?"

"They're for you. It was Uncle's wish." Malcolm's abruptness was becoming familiar to her, and she no longer felt he was being deliberately rude.

Dr. Jamieson's legacy to her was carefully stowed in a cardboard box, and when she lifted the first book she gasped and then quickly removed the next five. "This is a complete set of the Lymond books!"

"I believe he met the author on one of his trips. There are also books on Egyptian hieroglyphics, and there, at the bottom, some lighter reading." A germ of humor brightened his myopic eyes. "Including *The Pictorial History of Etruscan Ceramics*." He paused for Lauren's soft chuckle.

"In fact, that book was open on his desk when we found him." He stopped as Lauren's eyes clouded. "I'm sorry."

"Don't be silly. He must have been concocting a new argument for me to research." She looked carefully around the room she'd spent so many happy hours in. "Malcolm, I really miss him."

"We all do." He cleared his throat. "Uncle Bernard directed us to allow you to choose anything else you want from the library. Go ahead and browse. I'm sorting in the attic if you need me."

Lauren felt like a cat choosing between cream and caviar. Books lined the shelves, endlessly fascinating choices, but she felt she had received most generously already. Her fingers brushed over first editions, leather-bound sets, lovingly worn tomes of historical analysis, and finally came to rest on exactly what she most wanted to read: Dr. Jamieson's personal journals of his years at the university and of his research and travels. If she could just borrow these to read, certainly not to keep, she would feel she still had a part of him. It seemed almost too much to ask, but she pulled them out anyway.

"What do you have there, Lauren?"

Twirling, her arms full of leather-bound diaries, she faced Chuck framed by the wide doorway. "I didn't hear you come in. Hi, Chuck." She smiled. "Malcolm said I should take whatever else I liked, but if . . ."

"I didn't mean to startle you." Chuck's smile disappeared when he saw the journals in her arms.

"I'd just like to read these," Lauren stammered. "Not keep, of course. I'm sure someone in your family will want them."

"Certainly, as long as we get them back," Chuck said graciously, putting her at ease.

Malcolm popped back in and asked cheerfully, "Is that all? The journals? We read most of those in high school. Go ahead and take them."

"Giving books away? How about the first edition Dickens? I'll take that!" Flynn jokingly added, materializing in the doorway.

"Sorry. That's promised to U of C's library."

Where had he come from? Lauren wondered wildly as the journals cascaded onto the floor. Carefully keeping her back to the door, she bent to retrieve the books and her composure. How could the sound of his voice affect her like this? She had been thinking about him too much, confused by her reaction to him.

"Lauren, let me do that," Chuck offered kindly.

"Thanks, but there's nothing to it." She swooped the diaries back into her arms, juggling them into order. "My one problem will be getting all this home. I came on the bus." Rising as gracefully as possible, she casually turned. "Flynn, how nice to see you again." Proud of her composure, she smiled up at him.

"Lauren, what a pleasant surprise." Again that almost overwhelming charm.

Malcolm's eyes narrowed slightly as he studied Flynn and Lauren. "Lauren's here to collect her legacy from Uncle Bernard."

"And so am I," cut in Chuck. "Where have you put the épées?"

Malcolm gestured toward the far end of the room, where a long case rested under leaded windows on the credenza.

"Take a look at these, Flynn. Antique. French. And as sharp as the day they were forged. I've been waiting a long time for equipment as good as this." Chuck's enthusiasm filled the room.

"You only got them because you've been fencing longer than I have. I got the ormolu clock," Malcolm retorted.

"Some second choice!"

"Listen, Chuck," Flynn cut into their banter. "You want to try those out?"

Chuck's eyes widened in delight. "You've time?"

"You're going to fence this afternoon, then." Malcolm sounded just a bit jealous. "I've got a little more work here, and then I've been summoned to Mother's."

"I wanted to save them for something really special, but I guess trying them out can't hurt." Chuck was completely engrossed in his new toys. He lifted one sword out and held it up in the classic salute. Sunlight glinted off the gleaming steel and refracted into every corner of the library.

Flynn watched the dancing light. It glinted in Lauren's hair, highlighting the honey-colored waves. It had actually been difficult not to call her too soon. But the Blackford case was too important not to move cautiously. So far, Taggart had no leads either.

He watched her studying the foil in Chuck's hand, her green eyes luminous with admiration. "You actually use those beautiful things to fight?" she asked disbelievingly.

"It's not exactly a fight," Flynn explained. "More an exercise in control. Want to see? We usually use one of the smaller university gyms."

"Oh, that would be . . ." Her face mirrored her desire. "But what about my books?"

"You could leave them here and pick them up another time," Malcolm suggested helpfully.

"I'll just put them in my car, and after the match I'll drive you home," Flynn stated flatly.

She didn't give him an argument, and Flynn lifted the box of books easily from the den floor. Chuck and Malcolm had evidently been more than generous with Lauren. They knew, even if she didn't, the value of some of those books. And surely Dr. Jamieson knew his collection of pottery books would have delighted any library. Would he have given her anything if he hadn't thought her trustworthy? He had been too shrewd to have been fooled for long; Flynn would have to believe that.

3 The gym was small and airless, its high windows covered by protective grids so stray balls wouldn't break them. Portable bleachers had been set up at the west end of the room, and Lauren went to sit on the middle tier. The floor was spongy under her heels and marked with large circles which she recognized from her cheerleading days as wrestling boundary lines. As with every gym she'd ever been in, there was the faint lingering smell of sweat—not unpleasant—but a nagging reminder that she hadn't continued her own workout program since she'd come to Chicago. She kept postponing finding a gym. Another priority always came to mind, which, probably more than her morning croissant, contributed to her sense of guilt.

Chuck came through the far door, épée case under one arm, mask and gloves clenched in the other hand. "You should try this sometime." He crossed to her, his voice echoing against the vaulted ceiling. "It's great fun, and a pretty good workout."

She slipped her shoes off and padded down the benches. Lifting a foil out of the case, she slashed a *Z* through the air, causing Chuck to jump back in mock alarm.

"A ringer. You've fenced before."

"No," she laughed in response. "But I've watched a lot of *Zorro* movies in my day."

She carefully laid the foil down. "These seem awfully sharp, even if the tips are buttoned."

"Because they're the real thing. Technically, a foil and a saber differ from an épée in that they are thrusting blades, while this can slash *and* thrust. Remember how Zorro could open a line of blood on a man's sleeve? That was done with the side of the blade, not the tip. There's more to fencing than running them through." His voice lowered to a pirate's grate. "Eh, my hearty?"

"Keep away from me wench, ye pirate scum!" roared Flynn, already crossing the gym floor. He strode steadily forward, purposeful, with the careful steps of a large cat. Pulling the close-fitting gloves over his long fingers, he flexed each one several times.

"That's why we wear these outfits, Lauren." He continued the conversation he must have overheard. "Just enough padding so that if someone gets careless, no one will get hurt."

She moved back to the center aisle as Chuck, his helmet in place, lifted the case to allow Flynn to formally choose his weapon.

Flynn slipped his helmet on, too, and made several slashes in the air, testing the weight and flexibility of the blade, rotating his wrist as if to make the handle rest more securely in his gloved hand.

Once they had chosen their épées, the two men faced each other silently and saluted, foil held up over the left shoulder then swished down and out to the right. Finally, the foils came up to engage between the two men.

Lauren leaned forward in the bleachers, enchanted by the graceful interplay of the swords. A mere tightening of a muscle or a flick of the wrist altered their position. A feint. Two steps to the side, as if each was performing an intricate solo dance connected only by the buttoned tips of the long slender swords. She could sense this routine was just that: a set pattern which the two tall, slender figures, almost wraithlike in their white fencing uniforms, gloves, and screened head protectors, followed as a warm-up.

The slow graceful pattern moved right and left, as first one man and then the other lunged forward to be easily parried aside. The glint of the foils was hypnotic, and Lauren relaxed back onto the bleacher behind her, lazily following the sword play. Chuck circled to the left and the pace picked up slightly. She concentrated on their feet; third position—heel, toe-heel, toe to advance; tight leaps to retreat.

Suddenly, the atmosphere tensed as one man executed a quick riposte and pressed the attack. Lauren's breath caught as she realized she had lost track of who was who. Their face masks hid their features, and since they were of equal height and weight, she no longer knew who was the attacker and who was the defender. Her hands grabbed at the bleacher as she pulled herself upright and involuntarily edged to the brink of the bleacher seat. This was no longer an intricate dance but a deadly serious chase. The attacker inched the other man slowly back toward the padded wall. Lauren's heart began to pound. Surely they had dueled many times before and no one had been hurt. Why did she feel as if the sword play was in dead earnest and that the man falling back so steadily was in deadly peril?

He shifted slightly to the right, giving himself a little more room to retreat. As he continued to back up, Lauren felt the scene lacked only flickering candles and flying capes. Her tension reached out to envelope them. Suddenly the fencers escalated their movements until she could no longer follow the foils, only the flashes of reflected light.

Just as suddenly, it was over. Her breath whooshed out in a great sigh of relief as the attacker's foil flew high into the air and he was left defenseless. The victor, who was only moments before the seemingly helpless victim, lifted his mask and laughed. "Much better, Chuck!"

"But not quite good enough." Chuck flung the reply like a gauntlet, then turned to retrieve his sword. When he joined Flynn and Lauren a moment later, his face flushed from exertion, he smiled and laughed, too. "Flynn is the uncontested master of the foil, but I've only been at it for about a year and don't have the experience of college competition. . . ." He grinned at his friend. "I am learning though, right, Flynn?"

Flynn brought his foil up and across his body, presenting the hilt to Chuck. "That you are. Your day will come. And soon, if today is any indication."

He turned to Lauren, perspiration curling his thick hair in wild disarray. A fleeting desire to smooth it off his forehead crossed her mind as he continued speaking. "We'll clean up and meet you in the coffee shop—one building over, in the basement."

Lauren had no difficulty finding the small restaurant, and sat sipping her tea contentedly, thinking how pleasantly the afternoon had passed: her surprise at hearing from Malcolm, whom she had liked much better at this second meeting, glimpsing the dry humor his uncle had enjoyed; her pleasure in the Dunnett books, each personally inscribed with a witty commentary to Bernard Jamieson by the author; her shock at seeing Flynn again and being invited to watch the fencing match.

Her pulse still raced a little from the tension she had felt watching Flynn and Chuck's exhibition. There had been something very exciting about their competition. It had been fierce, sometimes so much so that it had actually frightened her, but in the end she had seen nothing except good-natured comradery.

Dr. Jamieson had so enjoyed Chuck's zest for life, and that side of him had come alive for Lauren during the match. Chuck's face had been ruddy with exertion, his eyes bright blue, and that sweet smile which held a hint of mischief had caused her to see a little of Dr. Jamieson in him. He was exactly as his uncle had described him. And so was Flynn. She had drawn pictures of him in her mind for months, and now she felt as if the two of them were far more than just acquaintances.

As the two men strolled toward her, she could no longer contain her enthusiasm. "That exhibition was so exciting! You two are good. For just a moment I forgot it was a friendly match."

"We take our fencing seriously. It's one of the few chances I get to exercise," Chuck explained.

"You're both superb. In fact, it was almost like watching an old Errol Flynn movie." She laughed.

An enigmatic glance passed between the two men, and for a moment she felt as if she'd stumbled onto a secret.

Flynn lifted a hand and a waitress appeared to fill his coffee cup. "None for me, thanks." Chuck shook his head and stood. "I've got an appointment downtown. I'll see you tomorrow, Flynn."

Chuck's face was flushed and his eyes so bright that now more than ever he looked like a golden choir boy. "Lauren, it was great seeing you. Glad you enjoyed our little exhibition."

Stirring her cooling tea, she said goodbye and watched him stride out. Flynn was studying her. "I hoped to call you this week," he said after Chuck was gone.

Feeling suddenly awkward, Lauren spoke quickly. "Yes, your handkerchief. I had it laundered." Again, vague misgivings tugged at her. "If I'd known you would be at Dr. Jamieson's, I would have brought it. Can I mail it to you?"

"Lauren." Three long fingers stilled her nervously stirring hand. "I didn't want to talk about my handkerchief. I don't want . . . I haven't had a free moment until today."

She did not move her hand away, and even relaxed it a little so his fingers could curl about it naturally. "Busy dispensing justice?" she questioned, her voice sounding slightly husky.

"Something like that," he said after a pause. "This case we're working on isn't going . . . quite as I had hoped."

There it was again, that look of caution.

What wasn't he telling her? "Want to talk about it? Dr. Jamieson always said I was a wonderful listener."

His cornflower-blue eyes flickered for an instant before he looked down and his long silky lashes veiled them. Releasing her hand, he sat back in his chair. "Thank you. But I don't want to begin our relationship by boring you silly."

Relationship. The way he casually dropped that word into the conversation startled her. He said it so matter-of-factly, as if there was no doubt about a continuing bond between them. Yet, despite her doubts, the seed of interest sown by Dr. Jamieson had taken root and was thriving. So now it wasn't like just meeting Flynn for the first time. It was more like recognition.

Realizing she had not answered him, Lauren smiled weakly, forcing herself to relax back into her chair. "I doubt it would be boring," she replied cautiously. "Dr. Jamieson never bored me, and we often talked about his nephews' work."

"Did you? I would have thought you two would discuss your common scholarly interests," he said mildly.

"We shared many interests," she returned, suddenly on the defensive. Why was that? Could he sense it also?

Flynn tilted his head, flashing his disarming smile. "As I hope we do, Lauren."

It was too smooth. She was right to be

nervous. Why would this man put her on guard so? They barely knew each other. Yet both times they'd talked she felt as if he was trying to learn something from her. And every time they got close to speaking naturally he would back away—as if *he* was frightened of something. Intriguing. Even appealing for some women. But not for her, not anymore.

"I've really enjoyed this afternoon. But I do have to get home. I have some research to do tonight." Her chair scraped the floor in her eagerness to get away from him.

There was some satisfaction in being the first to step back, moving away from his smile and light flirtatious words. Even though his lawyerlike tone unnerved her, a part of her couldn't help but be flattered by all this attention. But it seemed almost as if they were playing a game, and Lauren had long ago lost any penchant for games.

The loud shrill of a car alarm greeted them as they stepped out into the early evening. The setting sun cast long shadows into the parking lot, obscuring the harried security guard who hovered in back of Flynn's gray BMW.

"Oh, there you are, Mr. Fitzgerald!" Relief was obvious in the guard's voice and on his face. "He didn't get anything. But I couldn't get a good look at him—the sun was in my eyes."

"That's all right, George." Flynn's eyes

narrowed as he shut off the alarm and fit the key into the trunk to open it. Her box of books sat alone and untouched. "Thank you. Everything is fine."

The guard nodded his head before moving away to check in a car that was stopped at the security cage.

Flynn threw his gym bag in before slamming the trunk.

"I'm glad there was no damage to your car." Lauren added thoughtfully, "All they would have gotten was my books."

He turned around, his eyes locking once more with hers, that strange light which changed the cornflower blue to azure again filling his gaze. "Yes," he murmured, "they'd only have gotten your books."

He watched from across a side street, half hidden by a tree. If the sun hadn't momentarily blinded the security man he might not have gotten away with it.

He had to get those journals. Sure, he'd shaken them out in the study, and he had even read them. But what if he had missed something? What if the old man had written something incriminating? In the days since Dr. Jamieson's death, he'd been through every closet, every drawer, every conceivable hiding place. Damn the old man, anyway. He'd have to go back through the house once more. It would be easier now that the clothes were packed away and the aunts and cousins had been in to take their precious pieces of bric-a-brac. Not one thing had left that house without his careful scrutiny.

But he had a nagging worry about those journals. He never should have let Lauren take more than the doctor had left her— she'd gotten plenty as it was. But he hadn't wanted to look greedy. You never want to look greedy; he'd learned that early on.

Now he watched as Lauren and Flynn walked around the car, talking earnestly. Those two might be a dangerous combination.

She's a pretty girl. He wondered what she'd been hanging around an old man like Dr. Jamieson for. She probably figured she could worm her way into a lonely old man's will. Everyone pretended that all they cared about was their friends or family, but that wasn't really true. All they cared about was looking after themselves. And women—they were the worst.

Why did the pretty ones always like Flynn, as if his looks or personality were superior? Yet women could be easily fooled with the right handling. You could either charm them or let them think they were saving you. He'd used both approaches in the past very successfully.

Squinting, he followed the BMW's exit from the parking lot. It would be easy enough to find out where she lived.

He'd come a long way, and he wasn't going to let anyone or anything impede him now. There were just a few more obstacles left.

Usually Flynn hated sitting in his office and waiting for an important call, but today he was glad for the time to think.

Having Taggart follow Lauren Michaels in the first place had been a long shot. Her ties to the Blackford case were tenuous at best, yet she had admitted discussing his cases with Dr. Jamieson. But she had done it so ingenuously, so innocently . . . it was next to impossible to still have any doubts about her. Still, he couldn't help but feel that Lauren was hiding something. Instinct—and wishful thinking, he admitted ruefully—told him it didn't have anything to do with Blackford, but he needed proof to back up his instincts, and if she had a secret, he wanted to know what it was.

He was ready when the phone finally rang. "Fitzgerald here. Taggart! Where in the hell have you been! I gave you strict instructions to watch . . ." Closing his eyes, Flynn leaned his head back on his swivel chair. "No, no, I didn't see you in the coffee shop." His lips curved in a wry smile. "Yes, that's right. You aren't suppose to let her out of your sight. Especially now."

He opened his eyes, raking his fingers through his already mussed hair. "I want you to find out everything there is to know about Lauren Michaels. Everything. Do you understand, Taggart? By the time you're finished I want to know every one of her secrets."

4 It was a delicious springlike day for Chicago in April, a time of year that more often than not was bitterly cold. Instead, a warm breeze off the lake offered a break from an unending winter, prompting Lauren to take the long route to work. She walked along the river to Michigan Avenue, then headed south toward the park. At seven-thirty in the morning the city was alive; bumper to bumper traffic, joggers on the lakefront, trucks anxious to make their deliveries and get out of the congestion. Stopping at a corner newsstand, she picked up a copy of the *Tribune*.

The vendor recognized her with a cheery salute. "Hey, pretty lady. Bet with this weather, I'll be seein' you every day now."

"I hope so. How's your wife?"

"She has her good days and bad. I'll tell her you asked."

"I've got a book she'll enjoy. Pictures of cats. I'll bring it tomorrow."

It was easy to be nice to people you didn't really know. People who didn't really know you. The ones you couldn't trust were the ones who wanted to know you better. They always wanted something. A flutter of awareness shivered up her spine. She swung around, certain someone was standing behind her, but no one was there. The vendor, startled, raised his bushy eyebrows. Lauren returned a smile, tucked the paper under her arm, and moved away.

Ahead, Buckingham Fountain threw its spray into the sky. As usual, Lauren stopped, squinting her eyes at the morning sun and imagining the colored lights of evening reflected in the water. So few natives appreciated this beauty right in the middle of their busy city.

There it was again.

Just a feeling, nothing more. But when she looked around, nobody was paying attention to her at all. She was imagining things.

Still, the feeling persisted, so instead of taking the path through the park, she decided to stick to the sidewalk. She dodged the jostling pedestrians, as impatient cabs rushed through the streetlights and car horns shrieked. Her pace increased, and by the time she reached the museum entrance she was panting from exertion.

The feeling hadn't disappeared, although she had given up looking behind her in an effort to catch unaware whoever was there. She entered the side door for employees only, and quickly looked out a window. No one.

Once inside the familiar cafeteria, she settled down to her usual routine: a croissant and juice, and the paper; it was just the thing to bring her back to reality. After skimming the front page, she chuckled through the local gossip column, devoured the comics, and found out the Cubs had lost again and were four games out of first place. Then, finally, she turned to the city news section. Chicago politics could always be counted on to be stimulating, if not downright amusing.

Her green eyes froze. There he was—front page—Flynn Fitzgerald. Her heart did a curious flip-flop. TOP PROSECUTOR FOILED AGAIN read the headline. The camera had caught him with a thoughtful smile. From their two brief encounters she already knew that smile, his professional face, designed to elicit confidence. Even a newspaper photo in fuzzy black and white caught the quality which so persistently drew her attention. And perhaps if she hadn't been studying the picture she would have missed the give-away, one hand whose fingers were clenched so tightly around a file that the white knuckles stood out.

That was it! The veneer suggested confidence and skill, firmness; but the man himself was vulnerable.

The headline drew her eye again. Another valuable witness had been lost in the

Blackford case. The suspect had skipped town before Flynn's office could even subpoena him.

Blackford was the biggest news story in Chicago. She remembered how upset Dr. Jamieson had been when the story first broke. He had rushed off to call his nephews, and when he returned his face had been grim. She had hesitated for a moment, then asked if there was really a grand jury investigation underway against Councilman Blackford, Chairman of the Ways and Means Committee for the city council. As was his way, Dr. Jamieson carefully explained that it was true, but that now that the media had found out about it, the whole case was somehow jeopardized. Malcolm and Chuck were very upset, he had told her, and Flynn was furious.

According to Dr. Jamieson, their office knew there were massive pay-offs being made to government officials to get lucrative building contracts in the city, and they knew it all centered around Councilman Blackford. All they had to do was get their witnesses in front of the grand jury—which was proving to be next to impossible. The witnesses kept disappearing—or suddenly refusing to cooperate. It didn't help, she supposed, that since Blackford had become aware of the investigation, he had been loudly declaring his innocence over every radio and television station in the city. Without proof, there was no case, and that

proof was apparently still eluding all of
them.

Lauren smiled at Flynn's picture, her
fingertip tracing his determined jawline.
The Fitzgerald Dr. Jamieson had described
wouldn't give up. Of that she was certain.

A nondescript gentleman of middle age,
stature, and coloring entered Flynn's office,
moving surprisingly quietly. His eyes
searched the room quickly, and finding only
Flynn, he suddenly seemed to grow two
inches, taking on a personality as well as
height. He removed his hat, revealing a
hawklike countenance.

"Taggart." Flynn smiled expectantly.
"You've got something for me."

Taggart's handshake was firm, his eyes
clear gray. "Nope." His head punctuated
the single word. "Left Larry at the museum
with her. I'm telling you, this kid's squeaky
clean."

A rush of relief surprised Flynn, but he
refused to give in to his emotions. "Taggart,
this is important." He firmed his voice.
"You've been on her only a week."

Taggart sat in the leather armchair facing the desk. "I've been doing this a lot of
years, and I tell you, this Lauren's okay. I've
even got a glass on her apartment. She
studies at night, meets nobody, goes to
work, and seems to have only one friend—
that supervisor of hers."

"How can a beautiful woman like Lauren Michaels have no friends?" Flynn frowned. That didn't sound right. Could she have a reason for keeping to herself?

"I don't know. She's only been here about eighteen months, according to her lease. Maybe she's shy."

Was it shyness which made her constantly retreat from him? Flynn didn't think so. And a year and a half was plenty of time to make friends—even in a big city. He pushed the swivel chair back from his desk and asked, "Where'd she come from?"

"Muncie, Indiana. I'm working on that right now. Should have something in a few days."

"All right. In the meantime, stick with her. There was another leak around the grand jury investigation against Blackford. The witness skipped town."

"I read about it in the paper." Taggart crossed one leg over the other and leaned forward. "Pretty soon she's gonna make me. She was really skittery this morning going to work."

"This could be it, then!" Flynn straightened his chair, relief turning into emotion of an entirely different kind. "Maybe she's nervous because she's making contact today."

"Flynn, you're off base on this. The girl pets strays. Helps old ladies across the street. Even buys her own flowers for her desk. You can only follow suspects for so long before they figure it out. This one is so naive we've lasted longer than usual.

"Pull back a bit then. And let me know the minute you get information out of Indiana."

Taggart gave him a long look. He paused, as if about to say something else, then apparently changed his mind and turned, leaving as quietly as he had entered.

Flynn swiveled to look out over the lake. He'd known Taggart a long time. If Taggart thought Flynn was wrong about Lauren Michaels, Taggart was probably right. Anyway, Flynn's gut instinct all along had been that this was a long shot. But Lauren was a puzzle, and he wouldn't rest until all the pieces fit together. Then, maybe, he could stop thinking about her. Maybe.

"Damn it, Flynn!" Chuck burst through the door just then, with Malcolm close behind him. Flynn whirled around to face them. "I just got a call from the mayor's office about the story in the *Trib*."

Flynn grimaced, motioning Chuck to sit down. "I got a call earlier. Makes me look like a fool, doesn't it?"

"The story makes you look incompetent," Malcolm said loudly.

Flynn looked up as Malcolm shut the office door behind him. Pushing his glasses higher on his nose, he slid into a chair next to Chuck. "The facts speak for themselves, of course," Malcolm continued. "As I said, you look incompetent."

"Thanks a lot, Malcolm!" snapped Chuck. "You're part of the team, you know. If Flynn looks incompetent, so do we."

"But Flynn's Chief of the Criminal Division," Malcolm reasoned. "The buck ultimately stops with him."

Chuck got a look in his eyes that usually heralded an argument between the two cousins, but Flynn stopped it. "Chuck, Malcolm's right."

"Hey, Flynn, we're a team. That's why we're so good." Chuck grinned, rising to his feet to pace around the room. "We've got to find out what's going on." Stopping before his cousin, he gave Malcolm his choirboy smile. "Any ideas, hot shot?"

"Follow all our leads, even the faintest ones. Maintain security. The logical choices, don't you think, Flynn?" Malcolm stated flatly.

Flynn smiled into his darkly stern face. Malcolm and Chuck sometimes acted like twin brothers out to prove how different they were. "Yeah, you're right. We've got to follow our leads. And our instincts. Something will come up."

Flynn chuckled to himself as his two pals filed out the door, peace restored between them. They each approached things differently, but both were sharp as tacks. Sometimes it seemed nothing much had changed since law school. Malcolm was still the doomsayer, constantly pointing out the worst scenarios, while working his hardest to prevent them. Chuck was the eternal optimist—there was nothing they couldn't tackle, nothing they couldn't accomplish if they worked hard enough.

And Flynn himself. His role was still the same; finding the middle ground and, usually, the solution to their problems.

But this time the problem was a big one; large-scale corruption in a city known for backroom deals. And now it was slipping out of their fingers. Somewhere, there was a leak. He'd gotten them out of messes before—even if they hadn't been as ugly. Now it was his job to pull them all out of this one.

Flynn glanced at his watch. Instinct urged him to take Malcolm's advice and follow even the faintest of leads. Incurably honest, he admitted to himself his motives in this case were not all related to his job. If he hurried, he should be at the museum just in time.

His plan was working. Flynn was definitely on the run, and by the time this case broke apart, his career would be in ruins.

At least all those years in law school hadn't been wasted. He knew how to destroy a case, as well as how to build one. He closed his office door and crossed purposefully to the desk. He opened the file with all the carefully compiled notes on Operation Blackford. Six major witnesses had come forward, and now, three were gone. The oth-

ers were beginning to get nervous. He ticked them off on his fingers. Without hard evidence, this one was going to end up all hearsay and innuendo, and he was going to do his best to make sure that Councilman Blackford came out smelling like a rose.

Soon he'd have friends in high places. Visions of the mayor's office, the governor's mansion, the White House danced fancifully through his daydreams. He smiled all the way down in the elevator to the coffee shop, where the public phone was located.

"Hello. . . . Patience, Councilman Blackford! Hasn't everything I promised you worked out?"

He stood with his back to the wall, presenting the appearance of a casual conversation, but his eyes constantly searched the small coffee shop for a spy. After this latest coup, he thought he deserved credit, instead of the complaints now being launched from the other end.

"Believe me," he interrupted the councilman's tirade, "I've already got a plan for that witness. Trust me."

The councilman was clearly nervous, and so he should be. He'd helped to build this case, and it was a good one. Only he was smart enough to know exactly how to pick it apart.

Good thing the councilman's people had come to him. And they'd offered him money. Ha! He'd taken a little in the beginning so their suspicions wouldn't be aroused. It was only lately that he'd begun hinting at what he truly wanted. Blackford had all the right connections. The Chicago political machine might be in need of a complete overhaul, but it was still in place, and a clever man like himself knew exactly how to use it.

One of the law clerks entered the coffee shop, and he ended the conversation abruptly.

Lauren spent most of the day trying to coordinate a joint seminar with one of the potters at the Art Institute. Getting one of the faculty members was no problem, they were always eager to help; the difficulty was scheduling a work room. Funds and space— never-ending problems for the museum. Fortunately, this time she'd found a solution.

She loved this place. When she was a freshman in college and her mother had insisted they drive in from Indiana to view King Tut's treasures, the trip had changed her life. She had switched to an archaelogy major and pursued a passionate interest in Egyptology. To be able to actually handle some of the ancient, priceless objects one day had become her dream. Even after she realized the dream—had studied and handled not only treasures, but pieces of earthenware and stone, shards of glass, bones, and rusty tools—Lauren still felt the overwhelming sense of wonder. Unlike some of her colleagues, she had no problem stepping out of her analytical view into her imagination.

She'd worked hard, earning the right to assist on a dig at Cheops' tomb; she'd been there when the first "ship of the dead" had been discovered intact. And now, after all the preparation—schools, digs, graduate courses—she was eager to share her knowledge and enthusiasm, especially with children. Children showed such promise; they hadn't learned to mask their true feelings or their intent.

Anxious to inform Bea that the pottery seminar was set, Lauren searched for her in the exhibit and in the basement storeroom. Then she climbed the stairs to the main floor and walked the length of Stanley Field Hall, dominated by the giant mastodons. She peered into the aisle exhibits—American Indians, hoofed mammals, reptiles, and birds—where Bea could often be found checking the cases, but she didn't see her. So Lauren continued up the circular stairway to the third floor office space.

When she arrived, slightly out of breath, she found Bea taking a coffee break over the paper. Lauren reached across the desk, picked up the *Chicagoland* section, and waved it tantalizingly.

"Bea, he's in here. The lawyer you wanted to know all about? Front page news."

Bea looked up from the stock reports

and blinked. Reaching out a hand, she said, "Let's see this paragon."

Lauren thrust the newspaper section back over her friend's cluttered desk. "I met him again last week at Dr. Jamieson's. I watched him fence, had coffee with him, and he took me home. He hasn't called me since." Lauren pressed her lips together, suddenly realizing she was babbling, but somehow she was relieved that she had finally told Bea about Flynn Fitzgerald.

Bea slowly hung her wire-rimmed glasses over the miniature sarcophagus, picked out in gold leaf and lapis, which adorned her desk. Raising the paper to within a few inches of her face, she peered at it closely. "Oh, my goodness, he is a handsome one, isn't he? Did you return his handkerchief when you saw him again?" She lifted her myopic eyes to Lauren's face.

Lauren smiled, shaking her head. "No. It's downstairs in my desk."

"Well, what are you waiting for? Why don't you call him or stop by his office to return it?"

"Bea, I couldn't do that!" Lauren moved restlessly to the table beneath the window where Bea kept a hot plate with a kettle of water simmering all day. Lauren poured steaming water over a tea bag, added sugar and let it steep for a moment before turning to face Bea. "I came to tell you the pottery seminar is all set. We're going to use the cafeteria. I checked with maintenance and promised to help with clean-up."

"Good work. You know, Lauren," Bea added with a twinkle in her eyes, "you're the only one who can ever get maintenance to bend the rules. Now why is that?"

"I suppose it's because I always help clean up." She sipped her tea, savoring the strong, sweet flavor of jasmine. "By the way, I left the first Lymond book, *Game of Kings*, in your mailbox. The other five books are on that makeshift shelf in my cubbyhole. Take them as you want."

"Thank you, dear. From everything you've told me about the novels, I'm looking forward to reading them. If they're only half as intriguing as you make them sound, I'm sure I won't be able to put them down. Which reminds me." Bea rose purposefully, replacing her glasses firmly upon her nose. "Those new pamphlets arrived. I'll get them for you."

"No, Bea, I can . . ."

"Stay!" Bea waved her hand dismissively. "Enjoy your tea. I'll take the elevator. I know just where they are in the supply room."

Lauren picked up the newspaper and did as she was told. Caffeine wasn't supposed to be soothing, but the hot, sweet tea made her feel warm and relaxed. So relaxed, in fact, that she slipped into Bea's chair, rocking gently back and forth until she found she could gaze at Flynn's picture without getting that nervous little flutter in her stomach.

"Lauren." Bea was back in the doorway, her arms full of crimson and orange pamphlets on pottery. "I don't know how he got in, because the doors closed five minutes ago, but he's here, wandering around the collection in the basement. Your Flynn Fitzgerald."

Without a word, Lauren was out of the chair and in the hall. She pressed the elevator button for the basement floor. When she emerged from the elevator, she spotted him immediately. She didn't want to miss him. He was inspecting a case of bronze and copper eating utensils. Lauren watched as he wandered over to the darkened tomb exhibit, and she saw him hesitate, smiling before stepping into the doorway and activating the light sensor. Instantly, the tomb was lit as if by bright sunlight. Everything was clearly visible: the walls covered with ancient drawings; the food, clothing, and personal belongings needed for the "journey of the dead" sat neatly in place; and there in the center, the sarcophagus of the pharaoh. Flynn stepped back, and immediately the tomb fell into darkness.

She came up behind him, intrigued by his intent concentration on the tomb. She gently touched his arm, stepping back when he twirled around, his eyes narrowed.

"Did I frighten you?" She couldn't stop her mouth from curling into a small smile.

His laughter was genuine, deep, rich, and Lauren realized with a strange ache, warmly appealing. "I confess. As a kid I thought the Field Museum was the scariest place I'd ever seen."

"Scary?" Lauren looked around at the familiar antiquities in genuine bewilderment. "All these wonderful relics of man's past, scary?"

Thrusting his hands into his pockets, he leaned back, tilting his head so he could smile at her bemused expression. "As a kid, I didn't appreciate their beauty. Remember all those awful movies on The Late Show? *The Curse of the Mummy. The Haunted Pharaoh's Tomb*. It's all here, down in the basement of the museum."

An absurd desire to brush aside a wave of graying hair which had fallen near his eyes made her thrust her own hands into her skirt pockets. "I would have thought you'd outgrown it by now, Flynn," she said with a smile.

"Yeah, I'm a big boy now." A rush of heat warmed her face as Flynn's eyes slowly traveled down her body. "You caught me off guard. But in fact I was thinking about you." His eyes stopped their journey and rose to meet hers. Their blue seemed brighter, lit from within.

She met his gaze squarely, even though the nervous little flutter was back in her stomach. "Why were you thinking about me?" she asked, hoping her voice sounded cool and controlled.

"Well, you still have my handkerchief."

Her mouth fell open in surprise—he had told her not to worry about returning it—but she quickly shut it. "Of course. I have it here in my office."

She didn't invite him to follow her, but he did; down the short hall and around the corner. His left eyebrow rose as he glanced around at the makeshift bookcase, battered oak desk, and lone chair.

"My real office is on the third floor. They're repainting it, new carpet"—She shrugged—"that kind of thing. This is just for a few weeks."

"Cramped, isn't it?" he commented.

Suddenly it did seem too small for both of them. She moved around her desk and hastily opened the top drawer, removing the flat square package. "Here you are." Only as she extended her hand across the desk did she notice the brown paper bag sitting squarely in the middle of it.

"It seems someone has left you a present." He sniffed the air appreciatively. "And one that smells appetizing at that."

"It's probably Kevin, the security guard. Sometimes when I work late I share my dinner with him. Or he brings pies his wife bakes." Opening the bag she peered inside. "That sweetie! Two chili-cheese dogs. My favorite! He must have gotten them before the cafeteria closed."

Now both eyebrows rose over Flynn's curious blue eyes, and one side of his firm mouth curled up. "Don't tell me that's your Friday night dinner."

"My turn to confess. I've eaten more hot dogs in the year and a half since I came to Chicago than I've eaten in my whole life. They taste better here. Would you like to try one?" The words were out before she realized she'd even formed the thought.

He stared at her for a heartbeat, darkness flickering across his eyes, before he slowly nodded. "Thank you, Lauren."

But not here, Lauren suddenly realized. Not here, in this tiny space which seemed to close around her even more with Flynn's presence. "The museum is shut, so why don't we eat out by the collection. I'll get some cold sodas. Meet you on the wooden bench by the mummies."

Flynn loosened his tie and with no hesitation unwrapped one half of the supper Kevin had brought her. Coming back from the soda machine, Lauren glimpsed a side of Fitzgerald she had imagined. Eating a chili-dog and leaning back, relaxed, he seemed more like the man who had been Dr. Jamieson's trusted friend.

"You know, I met him on this bench," Lauren said quietly, setting down the cans. "Dr. Jamieson."

Their gaze met, and for the first time his clear jewel eyes were readable. Hypnotized by the gentleness and sadness there, Lauren couldn't look away, even when his eyes darkened to deep sapphire. Her lips parted softly, a warm sensation flooding over her.

"He used to sit here between the hieroglyphics and the Etruscan pottery to reflect. He told me it gave him a sense of peace to know that history was being preserved." Lauren licked her lips, shifting her weight on the hard bench. "It didn't seem so peaceful to me. Almost every time I saw him, there would be a stranger asking him to explain something."

Flynn considered her carefully. "Perhaps he just liked visiting you."

"Not at first. This was a habit long before I came here. It took me a while to work up enough courage to disturb him." She smiled broadly, remembering. "Then he became a real friend. Although I didn't know how many other friends he had. I thought he was as lonely as I . . ." The words died on her lips. She was uncomfortable with the thought of appealing to Flynn for sympathy. Yet she had begun to do so without even thinking.

"Lonely. We can't have that." Flynn's large warm hand reached out to cover hers. "I'd like to be your friend, too." And then his serious tone changed to one of light banter. "I took an archaelogy class in college." He leaned back, clasped his hands behind his head, and grinned, suddenly looking like a young boy. "We could talk about that."

Her hand turned over, almost of its own

volition, to clasp his. "Yes, that would be nice," she said carefully, an unfamiliar longing overwhelming her. Caution, she thought, and gently she withdrew her hand.

"We could even discuss whatever you and Dr. Jamieson talked about," he added.

"I'm not sure you'd want to." She laughed uneasily. "Clay techniques just don't seem to be your style."

He straightened, seeming to tower over her on the little bench. "No. But I like museums."

Nodding, she looked around at the collection. "I love this place! It has so much more to offer than my old museum in Muncie."

To her surprise, when she met his eyes again, he lowered his to stuff their sandwich wrappers into the brown bag. "Yeah." Suddenly he looked up, watching her with that intent gaze that brought the heaviness to her chest. "Lauren, I . . ." Then he stopped, as approaching footsteps echoed on the marble floor.

"Excuse me, Miss Michaels. Time to turn on the security system."

Shaken, she tore her eyes away from Flynn's face and looked up at the security guard.

"Kevin, thank you for the hot dogs. I shared them with a friend. . . . Flynn, this is Kevin Lawrence, the night security guard for this wing," she said, smiling to calm her thoughts.

They nodded at one another, and Kevin gave her his slow grin. "Knew they were your favorite. Thought you might be working late on your pottery seminar again. You gonna be here much later tonight, or can I code the alarms now?"

"No, the seminar's all set, finally. We'll be going in just a few minutes. Thanks again for supper."

He nodded his balding head and moved back toward the stairs.

"Well . . . we'd better go." Lauren stood, uncertain and growing uneasy at Flynn's sudden silence.

He rose to his feet, facing her, and smiled—a genuine smile which reached his eyes, lighting them. "Thanks for dinner. I'll drive you home."

When he opened the door of the BMW for her she smiled faintly. He couldn't shake the feeling that she was frightened of him. But why, unless she had something to hide? Pushing that thought away, he climbed in and started the engine.

"I appreciate the lift, Flynn," she said quietly, not looking at him.

Trying to keep his voice very gentle, he told her, "Hey, it's the least I can do after you bought dinner."

She laughed softly, and Flynn sensed her relaxing back into the seat. He knew the route to her apartment from the last time they'd seen each other.

It was an older apartment building, narrow, with an elegant facade dating back to the thirties, sandwiched in between newer concrete-slab highrises. The neighborhood just off Monroe Street wasn't the best, but it was slowly being gentrified, and there were signs of renovation everywhere, even on the street itself, where barricades made it difficult to park.

Flynn was fortunate enough to find a parking place in front, and Lauren had her door open before he could get out of the car.

When he caught up with her at the front door of the apartment building, she turned to him. For the first time he noticed her eyes weren't just green; they had specks of rust. Her skin, despite the dry, cold winter, was a pale, dewy gold, as if it picked up the reflected light from her hair.

"Thanks, Flynn. Good night."

Suddenly he had the greatest urge to take her arm, to stop her from leaving him. This didn't feel right to him—letting her go without . . . he didn't even know himself. But there was really nothing to do except watch until he saw the security lock click shut behind her.

In frustration, Flynn slammed the door of his BMW and slapped the steering wheel with the palm of his hand. He had gone to the museum with the hope of another opportunity to question Lauren. But then he hadn't seized it. He only wanted to get to know her, Dr. Jamieson's Lauren. He didn't want to find any other Lauren, one that had secrets to hide. It was getting too familiar, this ache he felt when he was around her. How could he be objective and still acknowledge his feelings? Damn, she couldn't be part of this business! She'd looked like an innocent little girl today, sitting on the bench, a speck of chili dotting her upper lip. He'd wanted to reach out a finger to wipe her soft skin, but luckily she had flicked it away with her tongue before he'd given himself away.

The car had crossed the LaSalle Bridge when the car phone buzzed him. "Fitzgerald here. . . . Taggart! What are you . . ." He twisted around to stare back toward Lauren's building. "I can't see from here! Call for a backup! I'll be there in two minutes."

5 His heartbeat pounded in his ears. That was just too close. He had lost track of time—and his temper, when he couldn't find anything. It had been pointless to rip the paintings off the walls, but it had given him some perverse satisfaction, although his hand still ached a little. Thank God he had paced to the windows, rubbing his sore fingers, in time to hear Flynn's car pull up. That had been a close call. Too close. He'd only just gotten out and around the corner when he heard the elevator. Stripping off the rubber surgical gloves, he tossed them into the incinerator and took the stairs. Carefully, he let himself out the service entrance, crossed an alley, and hailed a cab, directing it to an address that brought it back onto her block. Flynn's car was still there. Had he gone in with her? And there were two squad cars, lights flashing, turning down the street. He smiled in pleasure.

Once again, he'd outsmarted them all. He hadn't been able to search her bedroom, but he had gone through the journals again. He

*was certain now that they contained noth-
ing incriminating. Let her read them to her
heart's content. In his perfect plan, this list
of Dr. Jamieson's was the only thing that
could give him away. Maybe it didn't exist.
But if it did—and Lauren had it . . .*

Pushing open the door to her apartment,
Lauren automatically reached to the left to
switch on the lights, but they were already
on. She stopped as if she had walked into
an invisible wall.

Stunned, she could only stand and stare
at what had once been her living room. Broken glass glistened on the small patches of
carpet visible beneath the tumbled books,
couch cushions, and overturned tables. Her
paintings had been torn from the walls so
violently that where a watercolor of sun-
flowers had once hung, the plaster was
shattered. Her apartment hadn't been lav-
ishly decorated, but she'd taken care in
buying each piece. Her favorite oriental col-
ors and dramatic textures had provided a
kind of elegant splendor to the small apartment which she had been proud of. Now, it
was destroyed.

She wasn't afraid, she told herself, taking two more steps into the ruin of her
apartment. She was confused and angry.
Why would anyone make such a mess,
throwing her books on the floor, turning
over chairs? Then she spotted the photo-
graph and her anger took on new life, her

hands trembling in fury as she lifted the frame from the carpet.

Hot tears stung her eyes. The delicate silver frame was bent, the glass so cracked that it distorted her mother's picture. One of the few things she had brought from her home in Indiana, the only memento that brought back good memories, and now it, too, was shattered. Why would anyone do this to her?

The furious tears calmed to a quiet sadness. She knew whoever had done this was gone. She could feel the silence, the emptiness close in around her. Once again, she would have to pick up the pieces and go on.

Moments later, although there was no sound, no scent, she knew she was no longer alone, and she whirled to face the open doorway, prepared to scream. But there was no intruder, only Flynn, tall and quiet, standing in the doorway. Relief coursed through her, making her light-headed. Without a word, she set the precious silver frame on a black lacquer end table, walked carefully around the overturned wing chair, picked her way through heaps of tumbled books, skirted a broken lamp, and went straight into his arms. They closed gently around her and she buried her face against his chest, his heartbeat beneath her lips.

"Are you all right?" His tone was sharp and his hands ran urgently from the slope of her shoulders to the small of her back.

Temptation relaxed her body even more

heavily into his. But sanity quickly placed her palms against his chest and pushed her away from him. She looked up into his clear blue eyes and blinked. If she wasn't so confused, she never would have gone to him so eagerly. "Flynn, what are you doing here?"

"Never mind that now, Lauren." He studied her drawn face and bewildered eyes. "Are you all right?" he demanded again.

"I'm okay. Can't say much for the apartment, though." She sighed deeply, gazing steadily into his stern face where a vein throbbed lightly along the line of his jaw. It had felt so good to be in his arms, even for that brief moment, almost as if her crazily tilting world had righted itself, as if here was someone she could depend on to set things right, to protect her.

"Whoever they were, they really wrecked the place." She reached for the textbook on Egyptian hieroglyphics that Dr. Jamieson had given her. It was open against the floor, its fragile leather spine straining.

"Don't touch that!" Flynn's fingers tightened on her arm, pulling her upright and almost back into his embrace. "Have you touched anything?"

"Only that silver picture frame. There, on the side table."

"All right. Just don't touch anything else. We have to dust for prints."

For just a moment she wondered at his authoritative air, then remembering his profession, she was grateful that he was there with her. He would know exactly what to do.

Flynn moved purposefully to the windows facing the street but hesitated a moment before pulling the drapes closed. Righting the wing chair, he motioned for her to sit down. "I've called for a backup. They should be here any minute."

"The police?" Lauren sank into the chair. "Flynn, when did you do that? Call them, I mean? And how did you get into the building again?"

"I wanted to ask you something, and someone else was going through the doors as I came back." He surveyed the wreckage, carefully picking up a newspaper to see what was beneath it. "Is anything missing?"

He was brushing her questions aside. Why? But she couldn't worry about that now. Forcing away her uneasiness about Flynn's sudden reappearance, she tried to focus on his queries.

"I haven't checked closely, but it doesn't look like anything's gone. The TV and stereo are still here."

It didn't look like an ordinary robbery to him, more like a systematic search that had yielded nothing to the frustrated searcher. What had they been looking for? Perhaps she knew, but one look at her face convinced him she had no more of an idea than he, and he wasn't going to say anything to frighten her any more than she already was. She must have been terrified to have thrown herself into his arms, considering how composed she normally was, and he could sense she'd been fighting for control ever since.

He glanced back at her before shouldering open the half-closed door to the bedroom. It looked exactly as she must have left it that morning—an antique patchwork quilt spread neatly over the double bed, the highly polished cherry dresser top uncluttered except for a small clay figurine and a bottle of perfume. The room was neat as a pin, a stark contrast to the living room, where the intruder hadn't held back.

"Lauren," he called. "He never made it to your bedroom. Everything looks fine in here."

The relief that filled her was absurd, knowing the thief hadn't pawed through her intimate clothing or searched her small store of jewelry. "I must have scared him off. The light was on. But if he heard me coming, how could he have gotten out?"

Flynn looked at her, his eyes narrowed in concentration, and when her words finally registered, she felt all the blood drain from her face. She wasn't a coward, but the thought of walking in on a burglary made her knees weak. She closed her eyes, fighting the desire to sit down. When she opened them again, he was kneeling in front of her chair.

"Lauren, it's all right." His warm hands covered her clenched fist, massaging it gently until it relaxed. "I won't let anyone hurt you. There's no other way out except the balcony and the door. Something else must have scared him. He was gone long before you got here," he told her, hoping it wasn't a lie.

"But he could have been on the balcony outside the bedroom, and gone down the fire escape." She heard the fear in her voice and tried to stop it.

Flynn must have heard it, too, for he leaned closer. "He wasn't here, Lauren. Someone would have seen him on the fire escape. . . . Don't be frightened. I'm not leaving you here alone. I'll take you to a hotel for the night."

She shook her head; the fear was conquered, only the anger remained. "Flynn, this is my home. I'm not going to allow whoever did this to force me to leave. That would make everything even worse."

Something flickered in his eyes as he moved even closer, and he spoke to her in a determined voice. "Then I'm not leaving you. I'm sleeping here tonight."

Her breath caught and her heart seemed to miss a beat. "You're being very kind," she whispered, her gaze clinging to his face.

Flynn made a sound almost like a groan and lifted his hand, moving his thumb to caress her jawline before slowly dragging it across her parted lips. Stunned by her reaction to his touch, she leaned even closer to him, drawn by her own need and by his eyes, which sparkled like jewels.

"Lauren, I . . ."

A loud knock pulled them apart. "Mr. Fitzgerald?" called a gruff male voice from the doorway.

In one fluid motion he rose and placed himself between her chair and the door. Two uniformed police entered the apartment, and a third was barely discernable in the hall.

"Yes, officers. I'm Fitzgerald. And this is Miss Michaels. We haven't touched anything but that silver frame." He gestured toward it. "Looks like our man was spooked. He didn't get beyond this room."

A heavyset policewoman knelt beside Lauren's chair. "I'm Officer Katherine O'Connell, Miss Michaels. I'd like to ask you some questions while the guys work in here. Could we sit somewhere else?"

Lauren glanced up at Flynn and he nodded. "Go on with Officer O'Connell. I'll handle everything in here."

Lauren rose to her feet and found to her relief that all the unsteadiness was gone. Before closing the bedroom door, she heard Flynn and the policemen commenting softly on the mess as they began their thorough and efficient dusting of her living room.

She pulled the quilt off one corner of her bed and gestured for the officer to sit. Then she sank onto the floor. "Why would anyone do this? I don't have anything valuable here."

Officer O'Connell nodded in sympathy. "Everyone feels violated at first . . . then angry, even vengeful." She hesitated, searching Lauren's bewildered face. "Is anything missing here?"

"Flynn . . . Mr. Fitzgerald said it looked like they didn't get to this room, but I'll check if you like."

She rose gracefully and crossed to the dresser, opening one drawer after another. Nothing seemed disturbed. Then she pulled out the drawer of her bedside table—the neat boxes containing jewelry and trinkets were still carefully arranged.

"Nothing's gone from here." She turned to look at the policewoman's surprisingly reassuring face. "I really didn't get a chance to check the other room. I did notice that none of the big stuff . . . TV, stereo . . . was gone." She stepped toward the door.

"Don't bother going in there yet." Officer O'Connell's voice stopped her. Lauren sat back on the floor and leaned against the wall. "It's always a mess when they're dusting. Now, can you tell me what happened?"

"I opened the door and found . . . that." Lauren waved vaguely toward the living room.

"And Mr. Fitzgerald . . . where was he?"

How had Flynn appeared on her doorstep at the exact moment she needed him most? And when did he call the police? Everything was so confusing. He had explained, and she wanted to believe him, but something wasn't right. It was as if he'd knew something had happened before he came to the door. But that wasn't possible. Stop it! she ordered herself. She was glad he had been there for her, glad, grateful. Everything else could no doubt be cleared up later.

Realizing that Officer O'Connell was still waiting for an answer, Lauren managed a smile. "I'm sorry, I guess I'm more shook up than I thought. What was the question again?"

"Where was Mr. Fitzgerald?" the policewoman repeated patiently.

"He had dropped me off downstairs. I came up alone."

"So you turned the key, opened the door, found the mess, and . . ."

"And I felt awful."

The policewoman looked up from her pad. "Of course," she said mildly. "Did you hear anything, sense anything?"

Lauren relaxed, resting her hands palms down upon the carpet.

"I was distracted. . . ." No, she really didn't want to go into her thoughts and feelings for Flynn. "I wasn't paying attention. I really can't remember anything unusual."

"All right. Sometimes if we push a little bit we can remember more. Just forget it for now. Maybe you'll come up with something later. If you do, call us."

There was a tap at the door before it was opened by the policeman who had been speaking with Flynn. "Kate, we're done in here for the moment."

Officer O'Connell looked expectantly at her partner.

"Not much. The guy probably wore gloves." He turned to Lauren. "Mr. Fitzgerald is straightening up. Care to check again if anything's missing?"

Once again, Lauren got up from the floor. She didn't want to face the mess in the living room. She didn't want to see Flynn and confront her feelings. She didn't want to answer any more questions. Suddenly, she was just plain tired. She wanted to be alone.

The living-room moldings and door jams were covered with gray powder. The residue clung to every surface, and some of it had spilled onto the rug. Flynn was calmly wiping the powder off individual books before setting them onto the clean bookcase. She was touched by his actions, and without meaning to, took a step toward him. The policeman held her back.

"Miss Michaels, we do have to fingerprint you. . . ."

"What!" All Lauren's convictions to be less naive, less trusting returned.

"Just to match with the few prints we did pick up," Officer O'Connell reassured her.

"No big deal, Lauren." Flynn smiling,

held up his hands, faint smudges evident on
all ten fingertips. "They took mine, too, even
though I told them I hadn't touched anything."

Reluctantly she submitted. Now all she
needed was a mug shot to complete her day.
Out loud she complained, "Since my apartment was broken into why, do *I* feel like a
criminal?"

Her outburst made her warm with embarrassment when Flynn and the officers
exchanged glances. She knew they weren't
to blame for any of this, but she felt confused and angry. If she was behaving badly
she really was sorry—Officer O'Connell had
been kind. But she had hoped never again
to have anything to do with the police. Whoever had done this to her had made that desire impossible to fulfill.

"We'll be going now, Miss Michaels,"
Katherine O'Connell said quietly. "But I'll
be in touch."

Lauren nodded, turning away as Flynn
showed them out.

Dejectedly, Lauren knelt on the floor. All
of Dr. Jamieson's journals had been rifled
through—and all of her history and archaeology books, a considerable number, had
been pulled off the shelves. To Lauren, that
just didn't make sense. Any burglar would
have grabbed the TV, VCR, and run. Why
would they rifle through her books?

"Flynn, thank you. You didn't need to do
this." She looked around the room until she

found the picture of her mother. Already he had removed the broken glass and straightened the frame as best he could. "You fixed my mom's picture." Her voice caught, and unable to stop them, tears began streaming down her face.

"You know, this is just a delayed reaction," he said quietly, moving closer, but not touching her. "Everything is fine now." A vein throbbed again along his jawline. She was beginning to recognize that sign of determination. "Why don't you go soak in a hot tub and get into bed? I'll make you some tea. I'm staying the night." The last flat statement brooked no refusal.

"The tea sounds wonderful," she agreed, ignoring the rest. She was not going to allow Flynn to babysit her, no matter how much he protested. But she'd deal with that later. For now, she was grateful for the company. And someone to help clean up the mess. "This place looks like a tornado went through it. I can't just leave it."

"You can and you will." He put his hands on her shoulders and marched her toward the bathroom. "Do what the DA orders."

She turned to argue, but the set of his mouth stopped her as much as her own weariness. She would soak in the tub and drink his tea, but then she would send him home. Just for these few minutes she would relax and give control over to Flynn.

The water steamed and the scent of jasmine permeated the air. With each bursting bubble Lauren felt the tension ease away. Flynn was right. She needed this bath to relax a little bit. Oddly, she wasn't uncomfortable being here in the bath knowing he was out in the living room straightening up. She hadn't felt this safe since she'd left home.

But she didn't want to think about that now, so she played the mind game she'd devised during the trial in Indiana. If a bad thought intruded, she forced it away by reciting the inscriptions from the tomb of King Tutankhamen. It had worked then, and it would work now. Good old Tut!

"When His Majesty arose as king, the temples of the gods and goddesses from Elephantine down to the marshes of the Delta were . . . having fallen into decay. Their shrines had fallen into ruin, having become mounds overgrown with weeds, their sanctuaries were like something that did not exist, their halls were a trodden path. . . . The gods were ignoring this land. If one sent an army to Djahy Syria in order to widen the borders of Egypt, no success of theirs came to pass. If one prayed to a god to ask something of him, in no wise did he come, and if one petitioned to a goddess in like manner, in no wise did she come. . . ."

It was as good as a mantra.

How could she worry about a little break-in, when Tut had dealt with the future of all civilization? Obviously, she should put things into perspective. Her problems were small compared to Flynn's difficulties with Operation Blackford, for instance. Yet he took the time to be here with her, to help her.

Lauren's skin was beginning to pucker, but she was relaxed. Stepping out of the tub, she toweled briskly, then slipped into her jade-green terrycloth robe.

She could hear Flynn whistling softly in the other room and peeked in to see him putting the cushions back in place on the couch. The room had just about been restored to its normal state. Why was he being so kind to her? She really shouldn't let him straighten up her apartment, she decided as she slipped into bed, and when he brought her the tea she'd tell him. But for now she was just happy to have him in the next room so that she wouldn't have to worry about anything.

A delayed reaction, he had said. That must be why her mind couldn't stay focused. She couldn't take it all in . . . not just yet, anyway.

By the time Flynn remembered the tea, the water had cooled, so he reheated it. Funny how he had lost track of time while picking up Lauren's apartment. At first, he had been puzzled by her strange reaction to the police's request for her fingerprints. Although he tried to put it down to nerves, a nagging doubt, had remained. But in cleaning up, he'd managed to dispel all doubts and regain his earlier conviction: Laura simply could not be the leak in the Blackford case. When everything was back in place he still hadn't heard anything from her. He hoped she was in bed, resting. She'd looked like she was ready to drop.

"I'm coming in, get under the covers," he called out before entering her bedroom.

Lauren lay snuggled fast asleep beneath the old-fashioned quilt. Flynn stood beside the bed for a long time watching the fine-boned features so delicately drawn. Her skin was beautifully translucent in the half-light spilling from the open door. God, she was beautiful. He wanted to reach down and caress the curve of her cheek, to plant kisses on her forehead, her eyes, her mouth.

It was difficult to accept the feelings Lauren stirred within him. He'd known many beautiful women, but none that stirred him as she did. He had thought Dr. Jamieson's rapturous descriptions of her were an old man's exaggerations—that a woman like that couldn't possibly exist—until tonight, when he stood in her apartment doorway and she had walked into his arms as if she belonged there. Then he touched the softness of her lips, and had been lost in the beauty of the expression in her eyes. Beautiful, bright, brave—even valiant—answering all the questions the police officers had asked her. Only afterward had Flynn seen Lauren wilt with fatigue.

Carefully, he bent over and touched one silken honey-gold curl which drifted across her cheek.

"Lauren, I'll make this up to you. I promise," he murmured.

Closing the bedroom door quietly, Flynn dropped onto the sofa, resting his head for a minute against the pillows. Threading his fingers through his already mussed hair, he closed his eyes, weariness becoming a dull, gnawing ache behind his eyelids.

Yes, Lauren was everything Dr. Jamieson had said and more. He trusted her. Tomorrow he would talk to her, and together they would begin to unravel what was happening.

6 Lauren woke abruptly to warm sunlight slanting across her quilt. She stared blankly around the room, trying to remember what was wrong. When the memory of the burglary returned, she moaned softly and snuggled more deeply under the covers. Last night she had been frightened and angry, but now she was only sad that she could never feel quite safe here again.

How could she have slept so soundly all night? Then she remembered Flynn. Sitting up, she shook her head and flung back the quilt. Her alarm clock showed it was still early. Quietly, she crossed the room and peered through the door. Flynn's coat was flung across the back of a chair. He was sprawled out on the sofa, one leg hanging over the armrest. Relieved that he was still there, and grateful that she wouldn't be spending the morning alone absorbed in her dark thoughts, she decided to cook him breakfast, a sort of thank-you for watching over her.

There was no need to wake him yet.

Twenty minutes later, Lauren was bathed and dressed in a turquoise sweatsuit, her hair shining. She felt presentable.

The living room was immaculate. It must have taken him hours to finish. And even though the books weren't where she would have put them, they were neatly arranged. The only incongruous note was the black wing tip shoes on the floor at the end of the couch. She walked around the end table quietly. He still lay fast asleep, one hand curled under his cheek. He had covered himself with the afghan her mother had crocheted for her, but during the night it had bunched down around his hips, leaving his bare chest exposed.

One bare foot thrust out from beneath it. She wondered what her mother would think of this. A man, and worse, an attorney, here in her apartment under the very afghan she'd made for her daughter. But what a very attractive man.

Sleep softened the strong planes of his face so that he looked young in contrast to the gray streaks at his temples. A little jolt of pleasure made her smile secretly. She'd never noticed how his thick eyelashes curled up at the ends, or how the firm corners of his mouth were curved in a perpetual smile.

She glanced down at his chest, lean and muscled, with a light matting of dark hair narrowing to his waist, which was hidden by the tangled covers. That little jolt tingled to her finger tips. She had an urge to touch him, feel his warmth. Involuntarily, she reached for him, then, shocked, she pulled her hand back, and in self-defense backed up three steps.

She cleared her throat softly.

"Flynn." His name was breathed on a sigh.

His eyelids tightened. He muttered something unintelligible and nestled his head more securely in the throw pillows.

She hated to do it. "Flynn," she said firmly.

This time his eyes opened, and an instant later he sat up, looking at her blankly. Blinking several times, he shook his head. "Lauren, I'm sorry. I meant to be up before you."

She smiled, and their eyes met for an instant of complete understanding before she looked away. Again, Lauren backed away three steps. "I put out fresh towels for you. If you want to take a shower, I'll fix breakfast."

"You don't . . ." he began.

"I know." She cut him off. "I want to. It's the least I can do to thank you for staying here last night."

He rose slowly to his feet and she turned discreetly toward the kitchen.

"I thought you'd be angry. I know you were planning to send me home before you fell asleep."

Nodding, she turned back to see him finishing a stretch: his muscles bunched, his arms outflung, his head thrown back in abandonment. She was glad she was across the room. Catching herself staring, she answered quickly, "You're right. But I'm not angry now, just hungry. Hurry."

Laughing, he picked up his white shirt, hung neatly over the back of a chair, and headed for the bath.

She stood for a few moments gazing after him, caught in the grip of some vague fantasy. Hurrying into the galley kitchen, she pushed him completely out of her thoughts and concentrated on finding something for breakfast. The refrigerator pickings were slim, but after surveying the contents, she decided she could whip up a cheese and mushroom omelet.

She heard the shower turn on.

Not even Flynn could be in two places at once, she decided. Knowing he was occupied in another room, she could function efficiently. She sliced the mushrooms, grated the cheese, and poured the eggs into the heated pan.

The shower went off.

Just as quickly, she was all thumbs trying to set the tiny table under the window with blue placemats and matching napkins. When she turned back to the stove, Flynn was there, carefully inverting the omelet in the pan. His dark hair was slicked back, still wet from the shower, but he had not been able to tame the unruly curl that fell onto his forehead.

"Hi!" His smile was warm and brightened his eyes. "Let me finish this for you. It smells wonderful."

"Okay. I'll get the juice. Grapefruit all right?" It seemed very strange to have a man helping in her tiny kitchen. "Coffee or tea?"

"Whatever you're having."

"Tea it is, then." She popped a pan of frozen croissants into the oven to brown, and pulled her special Earl Grey tea out of the cupboard. By the time the tea was brewed, everything else was ready.

"Breakfast is served," Flynn presented the omelet pan with a flourish and sat across from her. "It's kind of nice to have someone to share the morning with."

Inadvertently, their knees brushed under the table. Lauren eased her legs away without looking at Flynn.

"It looks pretty good." She wanted to avoid thinking about what he had just said. Keep it light, keep it simple.

"All I did was flip the pan." He laughed. "I'm pretty good at that. I was a sorority waiter in college, and sometimes on Sundays we'd cook pancakes for the house."

"Well, you flipped the pan at just the right moment. What else did you learn in college?"

"I learned that most successful endeavors come about because of team effort. And

I think we could make a pretty great team, Lauren."

She looked up from her plate, but the expression in his eyes was lost in the sun shining through the window. Was it possible to hope that they could become more than friends?

He watched her slanted green eyes grow wider, and they told him everything about her. Now that they knew each other a little better, he found it amazing that he could have suspected her, however remotely. She was so open and honest, her feelings playing clearly across her face. It had been a very long time since he worried about whether or not a woman found him as attractive as he found her. He hoped what he saw on Lauren's face wasn't just his own wishful thinking.

She shifted under his regard and their knees touched again. This time she did not move away.

"Would you like some more tea?" The sun clouded over, and for just a moment the true brilliance of his eyes emerged. For some reason, she couldn't hold his gaze any longer. When the sun re-emerged, his face disappeared behind the brightness again.

Before he could even answer, she rose from the table to carry her plate to the sink.

"I'm going to help." He said it in the same tone he'd used the night before, the voice that brooked no refusal.

When she turned to agree, she found he,

too, had risen from the table and was standing right behind her. Without her usual heels, the top of her head came to no higher than his shoulder. She found herself looking straight at his chest, and made the unsettling discovery that his shirt was open several buttons, revealing a tuft of dark hair laced with gray.

He reached toward her, his hand finding the soft curve of her cheek, and he stroked it once, lightly. Then he gently dragged his thumb over her pouting lower lip. He was so close, so very close to her, that she could smell her soap intermingled with the undeniably male scent of him. His breath was like a warm caress in her hair.

Her lips parted slightly and his mouth came down on her softly, barely stroking the openness. Unprepared for the pounding sweetness of his kiss, she sighed aloud. He lifted his lips to her cheek, nibbling around her jawline before his mouth returned to hers, this time with urgency, his hands dropping to circle her waist.

She swayed with him, feeling as if the very foundation moved under her feet. Somehow her palms found their way inside his shirt to the heat of his chest. It felt so right, so good to be touched and held so close, his warmth penetrating her.

Then she heard a sound. Not bells, although for a crazy instant she thought that at first. It was an insistent, persistent beeping. Gently, she pushed herself out of his arms. The real world had intruded. How had she let it get this far? Far enough that his eyes were dilated to a deep navy and her hands were trembling. "I hear your beeper," she whispered.

Flynn's hand stroked her hair, reluctant to break contact. "I know. I suppose I'd better see what's up."

With a few long strides he crossed to the desk in the living room, and Lauren slumped gratefully against the counter. Her blood pounded, not only in her chest, but at every point of her body that had rested against Flynn. She had wanted to kiss him, she admitted, but she had not expected this aching tenderness. It was as if she had never been kissed before. She knew she had never felt longing like this; his kiss tempted her beyond reason.

Anxious for a return to normalcy, she stacked the dishes in the dishwasher, and with automatic movements cleaned the kitchen. She could hear Flynn's low murmurs on the phone. When he slammed the receiver down, she winced softly, with the irrational feeling that the action had been directed at her.

"Is anything wrong?" she asked. One look at his face gave her the answer.

"It was Chuck. The contractor we were going to subpoena Monday had a convenient fire. All his papers were lost. Damn! How do they find out?" His eyes had lost all their warmth, and his body was rigid with tension. "I have to go, Lauren." He shrugged into his jacket. "Thanks for breakfast."

Although she had the absurd wish that he would hold her, kiss her again, she stifled it and hurried past him to the door. Maybe it was better this way. She wasn't quite ready to allow all her feelings into the open.

Stopping in the doorway, Flynn looked ruefully into her eyes.

"I'm sorry about this. The day started out so well. Could I see you tonight?" He rushed on, as if he were nervous. "I have a law association dinner I have to go to. That will be a bore, but afterward we could do something special. There's something I want to talk to you about. I know tonight is short notice. . . ."

She stopped his rush of words with a brilliant smile. "Tonight is fine. What time?"

"I'll pick you up about six-thirty. Oh—and it's black tie."

"See you then," she said softly, shutting the door behind him.

"Double-lock this," came the muffled command from outside.

Grinning, she slid the bolt home. Taking a deep breath, Lauren leaned back against the door, her pulse racing. A date! She had a real date with Flynn. He wanted to be alone with her, to talk to her. It seemed forever since she'd felt this excitement and anticipation, like a giddy teenager asked out by the boy on whom she had a secret crush.

"I don't care what you say—there's still enough evidence to indict." Councilman Blackford leaned back in his massive black leather chair, pursed his lips, and touched the tips of his fingers together. The paneled walls of his office were cluttered with photographs of important personages, attesting to his long tenure and success. He looked up at the picture of him with Vice President Bush as if to reassure himself of his power. Smiling grimly, he added, *"And if I get convicted, you're nowhere."*

His visitor smiled reassuringly. *"You know I won't let that happen. As I've said before, you just have to trust me."*

"You're sure no one knows you're here."

"We're in and out of city hall all the time. If they ask, I'll say I was following up on a hunch." He smiled with smug satisfaction. Everything was going exactly as planned. Even the mess-up with his uncle—which could have been disastrous—seemed to have left no serious ramifications.

"That Fitzgerald guy is pretty smart. How long do you think you can keep fooling him?"

"For as long as it takes. Nobody's ever going to suspect me. People see what they want to see." He shifted in the hard chair, not wanting to broach the real reason he'd

risked a meeting here in Blackford's office. "However, there is one slight problem."

Blackford's head jerked up at that. "Problem?"

"Before my eminent uncle died, he called to say he'd figured out I'd been using him as a courier. He stashed some evidence, and I can't find it."

"What? Am I on it?" Blackford flushed and rose up from behind the huge walnut desk.

"Relax. It's just me." He leaned back and nonchalantly crossed one leg over the other. "You're already in enough trouble with this grand jury investigation."

"But . . . but . . ." The big man behind the desk sputtered, collapsing back in his chair.

"I need only one thing from you: Pressure on the mayor and in the press to get your case to the grand jury before that piece of paper shows up. You know how the game is played. Force their hand. You have nothing to hide, remember?"

The councilman's face flushed red as he picked up a silver letter opener, gripping it as if it were a weapon of defense. "I don't want a trial!"

He was back in control again, where he needed to be. "Of course not. The D.A. is nowhere near ready to go to trial, and after today, the case will be in even worse shape."

The councilman held up his hand for silence. "I don't want to know. Do what you have to do, but get Fitzgerald off my back."

"*Off your back and out of office. That suits us both fine, I think. Just keep up the pressure on the mayor. After all, he is your friend. And you're innocent until proven guilty, right?*" He nodded in satisfaction. "*It'll never get to that.*"

"*Why do you want me to push the case up? My lawyer says the longer it takes the better. I'm not sure . . .*"

"*You better pay attention to* this *lawyer instead of Denis.*" He stood, pointing a finger at his own chest. "*I know exactly how the case is being prepared. I know all the witnesses. By the time we get to trial, they'll all have changed their stories, believe me!*"

"*Okay, okay.*" Blackford rose, too, and reached his fleshy hand across the desk. "*I know we've got a deal.*" They shook hands. "*I'll talk to the mayor this afternoon.*"

A soft buzz sounded and the councilman quickly picked up his phone. "*Denis here already! Get him some coffee.*" He hung up. "*You've got to get out of here. My lawyer is coming in.*"

The visitor stepped through the side door, very pleased with himself. If the mayor came down hard on Flynn, that might fluster him just enough so he couldn't think straight. Although he'd acted confident in front of Blackford, Flynn was proving to be more resilient and resourceful than he'd imagined. Keeping him off balance and away from Lauren, that was the key.

He found a pay phone and stopped. Intimidation, the part he really enjoyed.

"Briarwood Construction," he said hoarsely, disguising his voice. "Let me talk to Mr. Briarwood." He hummed tunelessly and pulled a small notebook from his pocket.

"Mr. Briarwood, this is a warning. Your friend Faber lost his office and records. He's seen the light. You better, too! Now . . . now . . . Mr. Briarwood, you have three lovely children," he glanced at his notes. "One at South High School, and the other two at Park Elementary. Your beautiful wife is at home alone all day. I'd hate to see anything happen to such a wonderful family. Understand? . . . Good."

He hung up the phone and strode away. Four witnesses down, two to go. Like lambs, it only takes one balker to cause them all to bolt.

Lauren took a cab to the museum, a rare luxury. Today she was in a hurry. There was so much to do before her date with Flynn. Bea would be so pleased that she was finally coming out of her self-imposed solitude. She'd been urging her, none too subtly, to go out for months.

She breezed into Bea's office without knocking.

"Guess who's got a date tonight?"

Bea looked up from the paper work on her desk. "Not you?" She smiled.

"Yes, me. And to a black tie dinner with the handsomest lawyer in town!"

Bea threw down her papers and pencil and fairly shouted with excitement. "Flynn Fitzgerald asked you for a date? When? Where? I want to hear every last detail."

Lauren sat in the overstuffed chair facing the desk while Bea automatically reached for the teapot and poured them each a cup.

"He took me home last night. And, Bea, you won't believe this, my apartment had been broken into."

"What!"

"It's all right. Nothing was taken. But, you know, that's the strange part." Lauren unconsciously smoothed her skirt. "I don't have anything worth breaking in for, really. But you'd think they'd at least take the TV or something."

"Nothing? Nothing was gone? How do you know someone was there, then?" Bea pushed her glasses down on the bridge of her nose and peered over them.

"That's the really strange part. The place was a mess, like someone had been searching it. I was really frightened."

"You were lucky Flynn was with you. What if you'd been alone and the burglar was still there?"

Lauren shifted uncomfortably in her chair. The nagging doubt resurfaced.

"Flynn wasn't with me. I mean, he

dropped me at the entrance. Then, after I discovered the place was a mess, he was just suddenly there."

Bea stared at her for a minute and then put down her cup of tea. "Lauren, you'd better start from the beginning and tell me the whole story."

Lauren dutifully recited the events of the previous night. Sensing Bea's growing concern, she ended the story without confiding that Flynn had spent the night.

"Well, maybe he was coming back to ask you out for tonight. I mean, that's what he said, isn't it?"

"Yes, Bea, I think you're right. He did say he wanted to tell me something and that somebody conveniently let him through the security door." She smiled ruefully. "Some security, if a burglar could get through it."

Bea shrugged. "Maybe you were unlucky. Did anyone else get hit in your building?"

"No, not that I know of. In fact, it's a pretty modest building, and up until now I don't think we've had any trouble."

Bea turned around to reach the teapot. "Have some more," she offered. "Well, if nothing's missing, I agree it doesn't make sense. You haven't had any big deliveries lately?" At Lauren's questioning glance she continued, "I mean, if someone was watching the building, maybe they thought you'd gotten something they wanted."

"Bea." Lauren laughed out loud. "The only new things I have in my apartment are Dr. Jamieson's books." She stopped abruptly and stared at Bea, confusion mingling with suspicion. After a few moments, she asked carefully, "I know some of his books were valuable, but not the ones he left to me. You don't think that could be . . . no, I mean, the books were thrown all over the floor, but they were all there."

"And not one of them has any value?"

"Only to me." She sipped her tea thoughtfully. "Can you actually imagine anyone besides a student or a scholar wanting *The Pictorial History of Etruscan Ceramics*?"

Bea threw her head back and laughed. "You know, it *is* rather a rare reference book. I suppose if I want to use it you'll let me. But some people have a thing about possessing rare books."

"Now you might have something there, Bea." Lauren put on a mock frown and spoke in a half-whisper. "Remember Professor Heinitz in the Research and Documentation Department? If he thought he needed a rare volume to complete his research, I suppose he might break into someone's apartment. I wonder if *he* knows about my valuable collection."

"Except that once he got in, he'd forget which book he was going to borrow and take them all."

Now they both laughed at their wild conjecture. Well known for his eccentricity, Professor Heinitz was a meek soul, and the epitome of the absentminded professor. It felt good to realize she had put last night in perspective. Considering all the good things that were happening in her life, she wasn't going to allow an attempted burglary to haunt her.

"No, the books have no value, except to me," she repeated, as much to herself as to Bea. "I'd never give them up to anyone, though."

"Well, I'm glad nothing was taken and you're all right. Lauren, you're just going to have to leave this to the police and assume that it was a random burglary." Bea strolled around her desk and perched precariously on the edge closest to Lauren. "You still haven't told me how you got the date."

A mischievous sparkle lit Lauren's eyes. "I know how you like to ferret out the details for yourself."

"So . . ."

"So, before he left"—Lauren decided to be strictly honest without, of course, mentioning the time—"he told me about this law dinner tonight and asked me to go with him." As dear as Bea was to her, she didn't tell her the best part; his promising they'd have some special time alone afterward.

"Have you decided what you're going to wear?" As Lauren woefully shook her head, Bea's enthusiasm filled the room. "I think you want something that will knock him dead!'' Taking one look at Lauren, who was mentally reviewing the contents of her closet—and rejecting every item in her wardrobe—Bea stood up. "That settles it. At lunch, we go shopping.''

Flynn swiveled his chair back and forth impatiently. Chuck and Malcolm, sitting across from him, signaled their concern to each other with unobtrusive glances.

"I know it looks bad, but we'll handle it together, just like we've always done.'' Chuck folded his hands together and leaned forward. "We've been in tight spots before, and we've always figured a way out.''

"Damn it!'' Flynn wasn't much given to cursing, but the situation with Blackford was becoming far more precarious than he had ever imagined.

"We have other witnesses, Flynn,'' Malcolm stated quietly.

"Yeah! But none as good as the ones we've lost. The case seems to be slipping away from us, and I don't like it one bit.''

"Perhaps we should take it to the FBI. They could tighten security. Or perhaps a mole . . .''

"Malcolm, you overestimate the FBI. They were in on this at the beginning. Still we've had leaks. I think Flynn is right. . . .''

The buzzer on Flynn's desk signaled a visitor.

"I want you both to think about this and

have suggestions ready for a Monday meeting. If we work together on this, as Chuck says, surely we can come up with some kind of plan. The grand jury can't be put off indefinitely. We'll have to give them something solid real soon, or Blackford will slip through our fingers. I'm going to subpoena Briarwood Construction ahead of schedule. He's the strongest weapon we have left." Flynn stood in dismissal.

Malcolm rose slowly, peering solemnly from behind his thick glasses. "I'm not sure the timing is right."

Chuck stepped forward confidently. "We'll handle it. Don't worry. See you tonight at the dinner."

"I'm looking forward to it," Flynn said. "I'm bringing Lauren."

"Uncle Bernard's Lauren?" Malcolm looked surprised. "I didn't realize you were seeing her."

Chuck stopped momentarily, his eyes narrowing as he studied Malcolm's face. "Now, when have we ever known who Flynn was dating?" He smiled at Flynn. "I think I'll have to steal a dance tonight."

The door to Flynn's office swung open and Taggart strode in, a pile of papers under his arm. Flynn was surprised by the intense expression on Taggart's normally placid face.

"See you tonight," he said absently to his assistants. He barely noticed as they rose and left the office, so intently was he studying Taggart's face.

Before Flynn could ask a question, Taggart gestured behind him.

"You'd better close the door."

"Taggart, you're acting like a private eye again." Flynn tried to lighten the atmosphere. But he did walk to the door, check outside, and then close it firmly. "So, what have you got for me?"

"It's about Lauren Michaels."

Flynn's chest tightened momentarily, but he managed to sit in his chair and looked almost calmly across the desk.

"What?" His voice was low and barely controlled.

"Well, looks like you were right. This stuff out of Indiana doesn't look too good for the girl."

"Taggart, for God's sake, what is it?"

"She was indicted on complicity in an investment embezzlement case in her hometown. I had trouble finding the info because the names were different."

Flynn's flat hand pounded the desktop in disbelief. "You mean, she's changed her name?

"No." Taggart looked at Flynn, confused by his unexpected anger. "You want this information or not?"

"Yes." Flynn's hand raked through his hair. "Yes, go ahead."

"It seems her stepfather was embezzling

and used Lauren as his bagman. She carried information . . . and money."

"Damn."

"But before you get too carried away, she was cleared on all charges." Taggart pulled out a file and shoved it across the desk. "It's all in there. Friend of mine put me onto the prosecutor down there. That guy is slime. Apparently, he was trying to make a name for himself with the case. He cozied up to the girl, then turned on her during the trial."

Flynn reached for the file but couldn't bring himself to open it. She couldn't be guilty of anything—she was too honest. But the prosecutor had doubted her—and used her. Flynn had doubted her, too, at the beginning. No longer. And he would never use her.

"What else?" he asked in a deceptively calm voice.

"I guess her innocence convinced the jury and everybody else that she had just been used. Nice stepfather, huh? Here's the kicker: Two months after the guy goes to prison, Lauren's mother drops dead of a stroke. Shortly after that, Lauren came up here."

"She was innocent," Flynn stated firmly, still not opening the file.

"But Flynn, this is just too close. Somebody's carrying information here. Somebody's working awfully hard to get Blackford off the hook. Maybe your suspicions were right about this girl."

Flynn looked at Taggart. "You were right and I was wrong. I know this girl better now. She would never be involved in something like this."

Taggart shot him an openly skeptical look.

"Flynn, you're not being objective, and you can't afford that. Not with something this big."

"I don't have to be objective. I know the truth. I know I can trust you that none of this will go beyond this room—not to anybody."

Taggart managed to look offended. "Geez, Flynn."

"Sorry. Thanks for getting the file." He swung his chair to look at the lake. It was gray and choppy. He heard the door open. "Taggart?"

"Yeah."

"Keep an eye on her. For her protection."

Carefully, he opened the file and studied the contents. Damn that sleazy prosecutor. No wonder she had been so leery and so jumpy with the police. But she had been declared innocent, he reminded himself, and what had happened then had no bearing now.

Except someone had broken into her apartment. A gut feeling told him all this had something to do with Operation Black-ford. Somehow, she was involved, but innocently; he'd stake his reputation on that. He *was* staking his reputation on it.

7

Bea was absolutely adamant: Lauren had to have a spectacular new dress for tonight. This was a side of Bea that Lauren had never suspected, but she allowed herself to be taken to Michigan Avenue for a brief shopping spree.

They started at Saks. Bea, who'd never seemed too fashion conscious, suddenly had very definite ideas on style. Several rejected dresses hung around them in the dressing room, and Lauren stood in a navy silk dress with a low, square neckline and a straight skirt that hugged her hips.

Bea peered over her glasses. "It has possibilities. We'll put it on hold for two hours. This is only our first stop."

Nieman-Marcus was a few blocks further north. Bea insisted she try on two dresses which were dreadfully expensive but fabulous. They rejected the first one immediately. Lauren stared at herself in the mirror draped in the second, a strapless cerise jersey which provocatively exposed a glimpse of her bosom.

Bea took off her glasses. "I think you look magnificent. This dress certainly is an attention-getter."

"Definitely!" Lauren tugged at the bodice. "I'd be a nervous wreck all night."

"Oh, well," Bea capitulated, disappointment blazing across her full face. "Maybe you aren't ready for this one just yet. Don't worry, we still haven't looked at Fields."

Marshall Fields, at Watertower Plaza, was one of the shopping wonders of the world, extremely busy as always. Yet Bea somehow managed to find someone to help them immediately. Before Lauren knew it, they had singled their choices down to a black-and-white organza creation. Lauren rather liked the way the ruffle stood up around her shoulders, but Bea still wasn't satisfied. "I don't know, Lauren. It's not bad . . . but I think we can do better."

"Bea, we've looked everywhere. As far as I'm concerned, it's between this dress and the one at Saks."

"Of course!" Bea turned Lauren around to unzip her. "I don't know why I didn't think of The Five Petals before."

"What's that?"

"It's a great boutique. The owner, Suzette, is the designer, and she's just a doll. Some of her dresses even make *me* look good." Bea chuckled.

Lauren fell in love with the aqua silk *chemise* at first sight. Its simple, fluid lines accentuated the soft curves of her body, and the scooped neck and spaghetti straps played up her graceful shoulders and slender arms. But it was the daring *V*, reaching almost to the waist at the back of the dress to expose a vast expanse of tawny skin, which had made her buy it. It was very simply elegant. And Suzette even took the time to whisk the dress into the back room for a few adjustments so it fit to perfection.

When Bea dropped Lauren off in front of her apartment building, she leaned over for a light embrace. "I'm so happy for you, Lauren." Settling back into her car, she winked. "Flynn Fitzgerald won't know what hit him. Have a great time!"

Lauren fully intended to. She hadn't known this kind of excitement for so long. Now she pirouetted slowly in front of the full-length mirror on her closet door, turning her head to watch the silk swirl around her thighs. She had bought an expensive pair of sheer hose and new shoes—ivory, watered-silk pumps. They were so delicate they looked as if they might last only one night—but it didn't matter. This was the night that mattered. After clipping on large mother-of-pearl and Austrian crystal earrings, she brushed her hair behind her ears so it fell in loose curls down her bare back. Then she gave her reflection one last inspection. Not too bad, she decided; in fact, she had never realized this color made her eyes appear greener.

She wanted everything to be perfect for

her first date with Flynn. Not only was she eager to see him again, but this was the first time they would spend several hours together. She thought she had detected a certain urgency in his voice when he mentioned having time to talk tonight, alone.

In fact, thoughts of Flynn had pushed everything else out of her mind, including her concern about the break-in. Burglaries were common, she reminded herself. She'd just chalk it up to the perils of big city living and forget it.

The buzzer rang and she sighed in relief. The waiting was over. There was no more time for vacillation about her appearance—he was here. She buzzed him up, then stepped into the bathroom to add one last spritz of Chanel No. 22.

She had imagined what he might look like in a tux, and she wasn't disappointed. He seemed even taller, the black jacket fitting his broad shoulders perfectly, and the pleated shirt emphasizing his blatant masculinity as he leaned against her door frame, smiling.

"You look beautiful, Lauren. Are you ready? I have a cab waiting downstairs."

"Just a minute." She turned away to reach for her purse. A sharp intake of breath brought her around.

Flynn's eyes were wide with mischief. "I like your dress."

She responded with a nervous laugh, a

blush warming her cheeks. "Thank you. I'm ready now."

They sat close together in the cab, his arm resting along the back of the seat behind her.

"Where's the BMW?"

"Parking's a hassle on Michigan Avenue. This'll make it easier to perform a quick getaway after dinner." Taking her hand, he held it loosely, twining their fingers together. "Don't forget, the date doesn't end with dinner."

Suddenly she couldn't keep her eyes off his lips, remembering how it had felt to be kissed by that mouth. Blinking several times, she nodded. "I haven't forgotten."

He smiled sweetly at her. What seemed like only moments later he said softly, "We're here." Releasing her hand, he slid over and helped her out.

Lauren had often stepped into the foyer of the Hilton Towers on her walk to the museum, speculating on how the crystal chandelier and lovely curved double staircase would look at night, filled with glamorous partygoers. Now she was one of them, and the scene was breathtaking.

Standing on every third step leading up to the ballroom, violinists played a soft, lilting melody. Yet the men and women talking in tight clusters virtually ignored them. Lauren ascended the staircase on clouds, her hand tucked firmly into Flynn's arm. This was the stuff of dreams: herself, in what she knew was the most becoming dress she'd ever worn; a handsome, charming, and successful man at her side; the elite of Chicago's professional society around her—lawyers, politicians, the rich, the powerful, those with old family names and the legacy of leadership, and some who had just recently fought their way to recognition. She recognized several members of the museum's Board of Directors. It would be a night she'd remember.

She caught a glimpse of a controversial reform councilman, surrounded even here by a television crew. But when one reporter spotted Flynn, he and his whole crew rushed over. Others from the media soon followed.

Flynn quickly turned to her. "Don't worry," he reassured with a wry smile, "this can be nerve-racking the first time. But you look beautiful."

The old memories flooded back over her when the spotlights flashed in her eyes. She felt trapped, caged in by the growing crowd. Relax, she willed herself. These reporters don't want anything from you.

"So, Mr. States Attorney, what seems to be the problem with Operation Blackford? You promised to clean up the city, and yet it seems you can't even get one indictment to stick."

"Now, Bill." Flynn smiled at the reporter who had just spoken and then looked straight into the camera. "This case is coming along, and I can assure you, our sources are doing their part. The grand jury investigating Councilman Blackford is only the first step in stopping the influence peddling and unjust awarding of contracts in this city."

Flynn seemed to relax a little when the reporters didn't press him.

But Lauren felt concerned when the reporter's sharp gaze fell on her. Flynn placed his arm loosely around her waist and she relaxed as he laughed.

"Don't believe everything you read in the paper. The investigation is coming along just fine."

At that moment, Lauren noticed a distinguished white-haired gentleman signaling to Flynn.

"Excuse us." As Flynn took hold of Lauren's elbow and propelled her toward the man, she could feel her tension ease away. Flynn must have sensed how she was feeling, for he leaned closer.

"Are you okay?" he whispered in her ear.

At her nod, he smiled. "Here's someone you have to meet. . . . Roger, good to see you." The men shook hands, and then again Flynn's arm encircled her waist. "Roger, I'd like you to meet Lauren Michaels. Lauren, this is Roger Farraday."

Roger took her hand, holding it firmly. "Lauren, glad you could be here tonight. Flynn, get this young woman a glass of champagne to help her survive your speech.''

With a sheepish grin, Flynn made a fast move to the bar and left Lauren looking questioningly at Roger.

"Flynn is making a speech tonight?"

"You didn't know he's the keynote speaker? Hey, don't look so concerned. He'll be fine. In law school we called him the great orator. He's got quite a career ahead of him, if he can just get through this Blackford thing." His voice dropped conspiratorially. "Can't understand it. I know Flynn. He wouldn't have called a grand jury unless he thought he had an excellent case. It almost seems like . . ."

Roger hesitated for a moment, as though he'd said too much. When Flynn returned with drinks, Roger added affably, "Hey, Flynn, I've got to find my wife. Nice to meet you, Lauren. See you at the table."

Twirling the champagne glass between her fingers, Lauren slanted a look at Flynn. "You didn't tell me you were speaking tonight."

Again, his intense regard brought warmth to her cheeks.

"Would you believe me if I said I forgot? All right then . . . how about, I wanted to be with you tonight and I was afraid you might not come if you knew. Are you angry?"

"No. And I'm not sorry I came." She stared down into the champagne bubbles rising in her glass. "It seems as if in the last few days I've seen so many sides of Flynn Fitzgerald. I think I'm beginning to understand why Dr. Jamieson was so fond of you."

She lifted her eyes to Flynn's face, and what she saw there caused her to cease breathing for an instant.

"I feel the same way about you." A crease appeared in his forehead and he took her hand. "Lauren, there are things . . . Damn! There's the call for dinner. We're going to get out of here as soon as we can escape. That's a promise!"

Flynn led her to the speaker's table, where she sat between him and Roger Farraday. Looking out at the sea of people in the ballroom, she spotted Malcolm and Chuck sitting at a nearby table. Chuck lifted his glass in salute, and Malcolm nodded his greeting.

Flynn noticed her smile in their direction. "I'm pretty lucky—my whole cheering section is here from the office."

He identified each of the lawyers and their spouses or dates. Lauren, warmed by his anecdotes about each of his cohorts, found new depths in him. Many of them had worked for him for several years, and she could tell that they not only respected him, but genuinely liked him. There was an easy comradery between all of them that seemed to rule out professional jealousy or any awkwardness between employee and employer. And each story Flynn told showed his high regard or personal relationship with the others in the DA's office. They talked of old cases and annual parties, mutual friends and colleagues; as well as personal triumphs and disasters. She sensed he was a man with true loyalty to his friends, a man who was completely trustworthy and aboveboard.

· Dinner was typical benefit fare—roast beef, scalloped potatoes, steamed garden vegetables, and strawberry shortcake with whipped cream for dessert—but still she had a marvelous time. Flynn and Roger kept her entertained with tales of old school antics, and Roger's wife, Carol, an elegant woman with a surprisingly sweet smile, joined in with some revealing stories about Flynn's prowess as a baby-sitter. Apparently, he was a great favorite with her three children. However, after a particularly amusing story about his encounter with a skateboard, Flynn laughed, put up one hand for silence, and stole Lauren away to the dance floor.

As they danced, his hand lingered on the bare skin of her back. The light pressure of his cool fingers caused her to step closely into his embrace.

His breath tickled her ear. "I've wanted to hold you all night."

They moved in unison as if they'd been practicing. He bent her into his arms, and she melted against his strength. Clear and sparkling, her eyes called to him; deep and fathomless, his eyes answered. The dance was over with a reckless twirl, and Lauren fell from her heights with a breathless laugh. How could one dance hold so much promise, so much meaning? Did he feel it, too?

Carol Farraday accompanied her to the powder room. She seemed very interested in Lauren, but discreetly declined from asking direct questions. Lauren was confused about it herself, confused and excited. As they re-entered the ballroom, the band was playing a fanfare and Roger was walking to the podium. As he reached the front of the room, the din died down, and he gripped the microphone and began speaking.

"Ladies and Gentlemen, welcome to the State of Illinois Law Association Dinner. As this year's program chairman, it is my honor to introduce our speaker for this evening. It was also my privilege to attend law school with him. I could tell you stories . . . but that's not why we're here. Suffice it to say that after being a practicing mechanical engineer for twelve years, I was unprepared for the life of a practicing lawyer. But E. Flynn Fitzgerald was there and, may I say, more than ready to adapt my conservative lifestyle to one more befitting a lawyer as dashing as his name."

He laughed sharply. "I'm prepared to divulge a little known fact tonight. Obviously our speaker's mother was a movie fan. How had she guessed little E. Flynn would grow up to be as swashbuckling as his namesake, Errol? I give you our crusading head of the Criminal Division of the State's Attorney's Office, Mr. Errol Flynn Fitzgerald.''

Flynn lifted one eyebrow in chagrin before rising slowly to his feet. "I'll get you for this, Roger,'' she heard him mutter before shaking Roger's hand and taking his place at the podium.

Carol leaned across her dinner partner and tapped Lauren's arm. "Errol? Even I never knew that.''

The mysterious *E* on the handkerchief had been explained. How could anyone's mother saddle them with a Hollywood name? She wondered what he really felt about it. No wonder he and Chuck had exchanged glances when she had remarked that their fencing reminded her of an Errol Flynn movie.

The audience had enjoyed the little joke at Flynn's expense, but before long they were all paying close attention to his speech.

Without directly alluding to Operation Blackford, he denounced political chicanery. His words were stirring and spoken with a conviction that captivated his audience with its intensity. Lauren noticed that even the waiters stood at the side walls listening attentively.

Beyond the deep resonance of his voice, Lauren didn't hear a word he said. Instead, she concentrated on the sharp planes of his face; how his smile promised mischief and then faded as he became serious, his eyes hardening. She studied the lone curl, frosted with silver, that habitually fell onto his forehead. Their dance had been a promise to keep. For the first time since the trial in Indiana she had looked into a man's face unshadowed by suspicion or greed, and felt a response deep within herself.

He gestured firmly, raising his hands to beckon the crowd to join his crusade. She watched the muscles of his arms pull the fabric of the dinner jacket across the outline of his shoulders. The pristine shirt and traditional bow tie enhanced his stark appeal. The rest of the audience might be caught up in the words. She was caught up by the man himself.

Thunderous applause startled Lauren out of her daydreams. Flynn was immediately swamped by reporters at the podium, and when the orchestra began playing a swinging rendition of "Satin Doll," Chuck appeared at her side.

"How about this dance, Lauren?" The muted light in the ballroom glistened in his golden hair. "It looks like Flynn's going to be tied up for a while. His speech on corruption and politics gets them every time."

Glancing at the podium, Lauren agreed, for Flynn was hemmed in not only by reporters, but by several other men who all seemed to be talking at once.

"Thank you, Chuck. I'd love to," she said, taking his outstretched hand.

He was a good dancer, although she felt a little nervous with his palm on her bare back. It wasn't the same as dancing with Flynn. Chuck didn't seem to notice as he kept up a steady and amusing stream of observations about the crowd. He knew all the important people and had a comment to make about each one. That famous judge wore a toupee. This socialite was rivaling Liz Taylor's record of failed marriages— and diets. The distinguished lawyer with the Paul Newman eyes wore colored contact lenses.

They had crossed all the way to the back of the room by the time the music stopped. She glanced over at Flynn, who was still surrounded.

"What did you think of Flynn's speech?" she temporized, moving toward the center of the floor, anxious to rejoin him.

"Flynn's quite a public speaker. That's one of the reasons he's gone so far, so quickly. He did a good job of glossing over the trouble with Operation Blackford, but he's probably taking the heat right now."

Lauren saw there were two cameras on Flynn. His outward expression remained calm, but even from the dance floor, she could recognize the firm set of his jaw as he fielded the reporters' questions.

"I take it from what I've read on it, the case isn't going well."

"Flynn hasn't said anything to you about it, then?" Chuck seemed surprised.

"No, we haven't discussed his work. But your uncle mentioned it often." She smiled up into his bright eyes. "I really feel I know all about you three because of Dr. Jamieson. He had such stories to tell."

"He often spoke of you to us." Chuck drew her back into his arms as the music started up again. "It's a shame we didn't meet before. . . ."

Flynn had said almost the identical words to her. How could one man speak magic and the other mean nothing to her?

Chuck tightened his hold when another couple caromed into them. "And which was your favorite of his stories?"

Before Lauren could answer, Malcolm appeared behind Chuck and tapped on his cousin's shoulder. The music changed once again to a slow waltz.

"I'm cutting in, if I may?"

Grimacing, Chuck stepped back. "Some things never change. Thanks, Lauren. I'll talk to you later."

With a wink, Chuck walked away, and Malcolm took her stiffly into his arms. He began a perfunctory two-step which Lauren quickly followed. Unlike his cousin, Malcolm did not make polite or witty conversation, but concentrated on the dance steps. As the dance went on, he surprisingly became less stiff and their steps less awkward, but still he spoke very little. When the waltz ended with a flourish, they did, too, as Malcolm bent her back in a slight dip.

Laughing, she looked into his dark face. "That was fun. Malcolm, you're an excellent dancer."

He pushed his glasses higher on his nose. "Thank you, Lauren." He led her toward the door. "How about a quiet drink? I could use a breather, and Flynn will be busy for a while."

Leaving the ballroom, they found the bar where earlier Flynn had gotten their champagne. Several couples had deserted the noisy ballroom and were enjoying quiet conversations nearby.

"Have you had a chance to look through Uncle Bernard's books yet?"

"Yes, and thanks. I've browsed through a few. The pottery books will be very helpful for an event I'm coordinating with the Art Institute." She sipped at the sweet aperitif Malcolm had insisted she try. Its warmth coursed through her system and then quickly expanded. She looked at the glass in wonder. "Quite a drink, this amaretto."

"My mother likes it. Thought you might, too." He lifted his glass. "I prefer scotch." After enjoying a swallow he continued, "About the books, Lauren . . ."

She looked inquiringly at him.

"If you should ever need to use Uncle's library, I'd be happy to let you in. The final disposition isn't until my Great-Aunt Matilda's son gets home from Africa and chooses his books. The rest are going to the university's library.''

"They'll have to devote a whole corner to him," Lauren commented with a chuckle.

Malcolm nodded his head in agreement and adjusted his glasses firmly on the bridge of his nose. "More than a corner—a whole room. I found stacks and stacks of reference books in the attic when I was rummaging through the house."

Flynn watched Lauren disappear through the door with Malcolm. At least she would be spared the worst of this, although, he had to admit, he'd invited this inquisition by refusing to change the subject of tonight's speech. All the networks had surrounded the podium, seizing the first chance to question him openly since the grand jury had begun to run into trouble.

The local station's rookie reporter had shoved his way to the front and stuck a microphone and camera right in Flynn's face. "What about the grand jury proceedings, Mr. Fitzgerald? Any chance they'll be discontinued, as Councilman Blackford has maintained all along?"

"Listen fellas, if you'll give me a chance, I'll make a statement everybody can use."

There was general shuffling while four

cameras were readied. Flynn waited until each team signaled go.

"I'm confident that the grand jury will move to indict Councilman Blackford," he began. "Although we seem to have run into some bad luck with our witnesses thus far, we do have more evidence which will be presented this week."

He smiled composedly, managing to catch every camera without trying to do so. "You realize that I can't divulge the nature of the evidence, but the people of Chicago can be confident that the District Attorney would not have allowed us to proceed without a strong case. The mayor has assured us his full consent and cooperation. He is determined to get the truth out in the open for all the people to examine."

"Are you saying that the mayor feels Councilman Blackford is guilty?" shouted one aggressive reporter.

"Mr. Lindly," Flynn addressed the reporter, "you know I can't put words in the mayor's mouth. According to our system, a man is presumed innocent . . ." Flynn's slight pause was enough to bring a murmur from the crowd. "The mayor is only interested in uncovering the truth of the situation."

"Are you pursuing the witness that skipped town?"

"I'm sorry, that's confidential."

"Isn't it awfully convenient that the very

records you subpoenaed were destroyed in a fire before the papers could be served?"

Flynn's chin jutted firmly forward. "These things happen. We do have irrefutable evidence which—I can only say again—will be presented within the week." His eyes darted through the crowd, challenging the questioners. "Now, if you please, I'd like to get back to the party."

"Flynn's signaling to us." Malcolm and Lauren had re-entered the ballroom, and now he led her through the thickening crowd to an unmarked side exit.

Flynn had her small beaded purse stuck in his tux pocket. "I'm not taking any chances on going back to the table," he said succinctly, resting both hands on her shoulders. "Thanks, Malcolm, for bringing Lauren to me."

Nodding, Malcolm looked quickly around. "Make your escape now, Flynn. The mayor's press secretary is headed this way. What'd you do—divulge state secrets? He looks pretty disturbed. I'll divert him. See you on Monday."

"I've had enough of crowds and reporters," Flynn said wearily. "I was hoping we could go somewhere quiet where we could be alone to talk."

"That sounds wonderful."

They were almost out the front door when she felt him tense, causing her to look around in surprise. Bearing down on them, a scowl accentuating the folds in his pudgy face, was Councilman Blackford. Lauren recognized him instantly from the pictures in the paper and television coverage.

"Skipping out on the banquet, eh?" He looked smug, and his words came out as a sneer.

Flynn stepped between her and Blackford, shielding her from his cutting sarcasm.

After looking cautiously around, Blackford lifted one beringed finger to poke at Flynn's chest. "Soon you'll be skipping out of town." His voice rose slightly. "If you know what's wise, young man, leave me alone, you hear? I've got a lot of power in this city. If you don't back down, you'll be sorry you ever started this investigation."

Flynn stood motionless, listening carefully until the tirade stopped. Councilman Blackford took one step forward, swaying on his feet, and Flynn motioned for the bell captain.

"Councilman, you're drunk," he said in a deceptively mild tone. "The bell captain will see you get home without hurting yourself or anyone else."

He turned away, the vein throbbing along his jaw line, and took Lauren's arm firmly.

A cab was waiting in front of the hotel. Sliding in, Flynn sighed and loosened his tie. "Glad that's over."

"Flynn, what about Councilman Blackford?" she couldn't keep from asking. The anger she felt between the two men had frightened her.

"Tonight, I don't want to think about that creep. Forget about him. He was just drunk." Drawing her close, he rubbed the curve of her cheek with his knuckles. "Where would you like to go now?"

There was something new in the air between them—excitement, anticipation. Lauren felt there was only one right answer.

Relaxing against his warmth, she smiled "Well, you said you wanted to talk. So, how about coffee at my place?"

Flynn unlocked the doors and Lauren turned on the small wall sconce and the lamp next to the couch.

"Make yourself comfortable. I'll only be a minute." As he filled the coffeepot, she could hear Flynn moving around the living room: She heard the drapes close and the stereo suddenly filled the apartment with soft music.

She reached for the glass mugs she kept on the top shelf, but only managed to push them completely out of her grasp. From behind her, an arm reached over and trapped her against the counter. She twisted around and saw Flynn's eyes lighten in amusement.

"You should ask for help, Lauren."

"I could hear you in the living room. I didn't want to disturb you."

"Well, I'm here now."

He deliberately leaned into her, shifting his weight seductively so that their bodies touched—hip to hip and chest to breast. Unnerved, she took the mugs from him and turned to the counter.

He let both hands trail gentle fingers down her bare back. "That has been a temptation all evening," he murmured into the nape of her neck.

Turning, she smiled up into his now serious face. She raised her hand and fingered his curl back into his hair.

"So? I've been tempted, too." She hesitated slightly before pressing her palm against his cheek.

Light seemed to flare in his eyes as he urged their bodies together. His mouth came down gently to hover over her waiting lips.

When he didn't immediately kiss her, her lids opened slowly. "Good," he breathed. "I want you to watch us kiss."

He kissed her fully, a tender pressure which reached inside her, unleashing a coiled spring. Her arms came up to hold him closer. With a shudder, his lips lifted to nibble tiny kisses from her temple to her throat.

The coffeepot's perking broke them apart, and his lips curved into a smile.

To cover the confusion, Lauren busied herself by pouring coffee into the mugs and placing them on a tray.

"Here, I'll take this," he insisted, and she followed him into the living room.

"Would you like me to open the drapes? The city lights look beautiful from here." She was chattering to cover her nervousness, and he smiled slowly, shaking his head.

"I like it like this. . . . Come sit down beside me."

This was a Flynn she hadn't seen before, and she found him very appealing. So appealing, that she slipped down easily beside him on the couch. When he handed her a cup of coffee she sipped slowly and let the warmth settle deep inside her. Their eyes met over the rim of the mug. The electricity she had felt earlier became tangible between them. He took the mug from her fingers and drew her into his arms.

She trembled.

His breath caught in anticipation.

"Lauren, I've been thinking about you all day. Of holding you in my arms . . . like this." His lips caressed her throat, and at last his mouth parted hers, the tip of his tongue tracing her sensitive contours.

Lauren was lost beneath his mouth's plundering. Her lips parted in tremulous wonder.

The shrill ring of the phone startled her so much that she gripped his shoulders even tighter.

Moaning softly against her lips, he drew back a little, his eyes sparkling like sapphires. He smiled into her bemused face. "I think there's a conspiracy going on."

"I'd better get it. Although I can't imagine who would call at this hour." On impulse, she pressed a soft kiss on his mouth before pushing herself off the couch.

"Hello . . . Kevin! What's wrong?"

Flynn heard the concern in her voice and came to stand next to her.

"The police! At the museum? Just what happened?"

Now Flynn leaned closer, and Lauren shifted the receiver so he could hear.

". . . Some kids vandalized your office on the third floor, Miss Michaels. Don't know how they got up there. Don't know if they took anything of yours. That's why I'm calling so late. I'm not here on Sunday. Thought you ought to know."

The sick anger and confusion she had felt when her apartment was broken into rushed back. "Kevin, you did the right thing by calling me."

"Miss Michaels, I know it's midnight and all. I wish you could come down here so we would know if they took anything of yours. But I wouldn't want you to come out alone at this time of night."

Lauren's eyes flew to Flynn's face and he nodded.

"Kevin, Mr. Fitzgerald is here with me. We'll be right there. I'll come to the employee's entrance. See you in about twenty minutes."

She dropped the receiver back into its holder and just stared at it. "I just don't understand why all of this is happening to me."

Flynn frowned. It was too much of a co-incidence. What did it all mean? "Lauren, let's get down there. Maybe we'll be able to figure it out."

She looked up at him. The Flynn of a few minutes ago was gone. This was the other Flynn, the man in control—cool and collected.

Kevin let them in through the employee's entrance near the Egyptian collection. He hadn't turned on any lights except in the main hallway, but those didn't reach here among the Etruscan and Egyptian antiquities. Seeing the displays in near darkness, the mummy case looking large and other-worldly among so many strange shadows, Lauren understood at last why Flynn had found the museum scary as a child. She had never realized how quiet and cold it was here at night. She shivered, and Flynn slid his arm protectively around her shoulders.

By now they had made their way to the lighted hall, and they took the elevator to the third floor.

Kevin shook his head, unlocking Lauren's office.

"The police said I'm not to clean up any-thing until they send someone tomorrow morning. But I thought you might be able to tell if anything is missing."

It was a bigger mess than her apartment had been. The smell of paint was overwhelming. On the plain cream walls, the vandals had thrown cans of brown and green paint, creating an almost surrealistic mural. The furniture—her desk and files and two chairs—had been moved into the center of the room and covered with plastic, which had obviously aggravated the intruders. Searching through her desk and her files, they had thrown books and papers everywhere. Reaching down, she picked up a file from the Ship of the Dead display and stuffed some loose papers back into it.

She took two steps into the room. It was like a déjà vu. Slowly she began to shake. Why was this happening? The mess in the apartment was one thing, but this really frightened her. Could it be the same person? How would anyone know she worked here? Maybe her feelings about being followed were right. The trembling became noticeable, and again, Flynn curled an arm tightly around her.

This time there had been a lot of wanton destruction. Somebody had taken out all their frustration at her expense. Lots of the files were destroyed by paint—months of diligent study and painstaking research lost in the mess. At least all her personal belongings, including several old maps of the excavations of King Tut's tomb, had been moved down to her cubby hole in the basement.

Pulling out of Flynn's soothing embrace, she circled the room in disbelief. "I can't really tell if anything's missing, Kevin." Shaking her head, she glanced back to the door where the men stood. "What a mess! There might have been some loose change, earrings—costume stuff. Mostly, I just had reports and files here." She nudged some loose papers with the toe of her shoe. "I'll have a heck of a job sorting through this."

"Miss Michaels, I've got to check the screens in the security room. I'll be right back to let you and Mr. Fitzgerald out."

Flynn moved to her side, and she snuggled into his embrace. "Flynn, do you think this is connected to my apartment burglary? It doesn't make sense, but something's going on." Grateful for his reassuring presence, she nestled even closer. "I think someone is following me," she confided at last.

Feeling him stiffen, she drew back, surprised by the lack of emotion on his face. A suspicion entered her mind, and she faced it. "You're not surprised, are you?"

"Lauren, I . . ."

"*You're* having me followed, aren't you? Because of my apartment . . . no, before that!" She stepped back two paces, and when he moved toward her, she shook her head, and he stopped. "Someone has been following me for weeks. Almost since Dr. Jamieson's memorial service."

His eyes widened in a way she had never seen—guilt or innocence?—and he threaded his fingers through his hair.

"I've had a man following you, Lauren, but if you'll only—"

"That's how you knew something was wrong in my apartment," she interrupted. "But how, unless . . ." Now her eyes widened. She remembered Flynn's preference for drapes closed against the night. Someone was watching her—in her apartment. The thought sickened her. "God, I've been stupid!"

"Yes, there's a glass on your apartment, but Lauren . . ."

Her heart was pounding so loudly in her ears that she could barely think. Once again, she'd been used. "Why?" she breathed, unable to quite take it all in.

"Lauren." He moved a step closer and she backed up all the way to the door frame, until he stopped and stood perfectly still, gazing steadily into her face. "You must understand. It's Operation Blackford. I thought you might have something to do with the information leaks."

Shock made her icy cold. Swallowing hard, she shook her head in disbelief. "Information leaks? But how?" Suddenly she put it together. "Dr. Jamieson. You thought he might have told me something and I . . ." The cold was suddenly replaced with white-hot anger. "Is that what all this has been about the last few weeks? Coffee . . . visits to the museum . . . spending the night to protect me. And tonight! So you could watch the suspect?"

He moved quickly, and she had nowhere to escape to. Even when he gripped her shoulders, his face grim, the vein throbbing along his jawline, she refused to look at him.

"At first . . . I don't know any more. I just know I was wrong. Then I thought maybe I could protect you. Something's going on here I don't understand." His hands let go of her, and he whirled away. "Even after Taggart found out about Indiana, I still knew you had nothing to do with it."

Fresh anger lent her strength, and she pushed past him to the door. "You've had my past investigated! My God, Flynn, how far were you going to take this? Was seduction next?"

"It isn't like that!" Moving swiftly, he reached her, his long fingers catching her chin, forcing her to look up at him. "I care about you."

Damn lawyers, anyway! How had she let it happen again? Every bit of anger and pain she had felt two years ago now strengthened the upward sweep of her arm. Her palm went numb as it struck his cheek.

"Miss Michaels!" Kevin's shocked voice broke the moment of absolute silence which fell as Lauren and Flynn stared at one another.

Somewhere behind her eyelids tears were burning. Not here, she told herself. She would never let him see how much he had hurt her. There was plenty of time for tears later.

"Miss Michaels, what . . . ?"

Flynn interrupted. "Kevin, take Miss Michaels to the cab. I had it wait," he said softly, his lips tightening.

She had an overwhelming urge to cry, rant, rave—anything to deny the betrayal. But she'd learned her lesson well the first time. She held on to her composure and did the only thing she could—she ran.

On the way to her apartment in the cab, it was almost as if she'd slipped back in time to the courtroom in Indiana. Her stepfather, sitting with his attorney and challenging her to defend herself, had hidden his guilt well. And her poor mother, torn between loyalties; the trial had literally broken her heart. Lauren had only herself to trust. Alone, she must figure out what was happening.

It had all started after Dr. Jamieson's death. The break-ins were tied together somehow. Even Flynn's car . . . and all that had been in his trunk were the books she'd gotten from Malcolm and Chuck: Dr. Jamieson's books on pottery and ancient cultures, his journals, the Lymond series, and several mystery novels. If something was in one of those books, someone wanted it pretty badly to have broken into the museum.

Yes, Dr. Jamieson was the key. Inadvertently, he'd drawn her into this nightmare.

8 "C'mon, Lauren, answer the phone!" Flynn muttered, frustration driving him crazy. This was the fifteenth ring of the tenth call he'd made since yesterday morning, and he wasn't going to give up. She had to listen to him. He let her have some time to herself last night to get used to the idea, but he never suspected she would refuse to talk to him. And now he was determined to make her understand the truth.

Glancing up as the door opened, Flynn felt mild surprise at the stunned looks on Malcolm and Chuck's faces. "What is it? Come in, and close the door."

"You look like you're ready to murder someone," Chuck commented, dropping into a chair. "What's Malcolm done now?"

Malcolm's narrowed eyes swept over his cousin. "Often, Chuck, you aren't amusing." He sank into the other chair, pushing his glasses higher on his nose. "Are you on hold, Flynn?"

"I think there's something wrong with the line." Taking a deep breath, Flynn placed the receiver back in its cradle. "Well, let's get down to business. I read your report, Chuck. It was very thorough, as always. But pinning the leak on the mayor's office is reaching, don't you think?"

Chuck bristled defensively. "There have been papers and memos sent between our offices constantly. We don't shred our papers. They don't either. People can be careless, even the best of us."

"But the staff involved with Operation Blackford is small," Malcolm interjected. Leaning forward, he laid a slim folder on the desk. "Here is the record of everyone even remotely connected to the case since the leak started. I suggest we study each person carefully."

"You know I've already done that, Malcolm," Chuck snapped, glaring at his cousin. "Are you suggesting that I've let someone slip through?"

Malcolm relaxed back into the chair. "No, I'm not suggesting you messed up. You're good, Chuck. You don't need me to tell you that. I'm suggesting we find out who—or how many—are leaking information. Or, stop the investigation until we do find out."

On some level, Flynn was paying attention to Malcolm and Chuck's bickering, but another part of him was detached, his thoughts centered on Lauren. Then he saw her name on the list.

"Malcolm!" Flynn's voice brought silence as both cousins snapped their attention to him. "Lauren Michaels is on this list."

He nodded. "I included her because of her close friendship with Uncle Bernard. I know they sometimes talked about our cases. He told me so himself." Malcolm turned an odd shade of red. "Uncle Bernard was my mentor . . . and Chuck's. And yours, Flynn. I know I discussed Blackford with him on several occasions after the first indictment. . . ."

"I did, too," Chuck cut in.

"So did I," Flynn added softly. "Bernard was the most honest, trustworthy . . . the finest man I've ever known. Although, perhaps you're right. I might have been more specific with him than I remember. . . ." Shaking his head, he glanced at both men and found them nodding in agreement.

"It's a long, long shot, Flynn," Malcolm soothed. "I don't really believe Lauren Michaels has anything to do with this."

"Me, either," Chuck added. "She seems to be as special as Uncle Bernard painted her."

"Yeah . . . you're right. She is special." Staring hard at both men, he could feel the vein in his jaw throbbing. "Do it, then. Chuck, I want you both to handle this personally. . . . Check every name on the list . . . except Lauren. Take her name off first."

"But, Flynn," Malcolm said emphatically. "You can't let anything slip through.

Getting this indictment on Blackford is a major step in your career. We all know that. And if you blow this, it will break you."

Chuck's usually smooth face grew hard. "I hate to say it, but Malcolm's right, Flynn. The pressure's really on, from the mayor and the media. You can't be too careful."

"She isn't involved," he repeated obstinately.

"Are you willing to risk your career on that?" Malcolm asked coldly.

"According to the two of you, I already am. You'd better get started. We'll meet as soon as you have something to report."

The look they exchanged was not lost on Flynn: he simply chose to ignore it.

Swerving his chair around, he gazed out onto the lake. There were two sailboats turning in the wind, one spinnaker bright red against the brilliant blue sky, the other aqua.

It was the color of the dress Lauren had worn the night before. He hadn't been able to take his eyes off her; the way it swirled around her legs, and dipped low exposing her back—that exquisitely smooth back which he'd longed to stroke all night. How had everything gone so wrong?

Now he was furious with one of his best friends for daring to put her name on a list of possible suspects. He, too, had suspected, and had gone so far as to have her tailed. But now he realized how stupidly he had behaved. Lauren was . . . Lauren. It was as simple as that. And he wanted her. That was worth risking everything.

Swerving back to the desk, he reached again for the phone. She had to be at the museum by now.

Lauren splashed more cold water on her face and looked in the mirror again. It hadn't helped. In fact, she looked worse than ever, her green eyes dull and red rimmed and scarlet splotches on her face. The bloodshot eyes were due as much to poring over Dr. Jamieson's journals as to weeping over Flynn.

The diaries had awakened the memory of how wonderfully kind and gentle he had been. They were full of his reminiscences of exotic times and places. A recurring theme was his utter devotion to Martha, his wife, and the importance of their nephews, Chuck and Malcolm—replacing the children they had not been able to have. That had brought tears to her eyes again. Devotion, loyalty, love—three things she could never hope to experience. The diaries were an insight into the workings of a brilliant mind. But they hadn't given her the slightest clue to what was happening now.

Maybe she should have called in sick today. After unplugging her phone—she'd known that the constant ringing was Flynn—she'd spent most of yesterday pacing, reading, and crying. She couldn't stand her own morose company another minute, so she'd gone to work. Bea would take one look at her and know something was wrong.

"My goodness, my dear child. What happened to you?" Bea put down *Queen's Play*, the second Lymond book, watching Lauren as she collapsed into a chair. "You need tea."

"Bea, I—"

"*Shh* . . . this will help. I put extra sugar in it." Perching on the edge of the desk, Bea smiled gently. "Lauren, I know it's awful about your office. I tried to call you at home early this morning as soon as I found out about it, but no one answered. I don't think this has anything to do with your apartment break-in, though. It was a vicious prank by some hoodlums. Do you know there was also paint damage in the hallway? They must have taken the cans and just thrown them around."

"It isn't just my office. Although, in a way, that did make everything clear to me at last." Sipping the sweet tea, Lauren looked away from Bea's kind face.

Bea's glance sharpened. "Made what everything clear? What are you talking about?"

"It wasn't quite the weekend I thought it would be. I won't be seeing Flynn again."

"Lauren, what happened?"

"I just realized that all lawyers are alike," Lauren replied bitterly. "Flynn's no different; he's a user, too." She fought to keep the tears from beginning again.

"What happened—" Shrilling right beside her, the phone startled Bea so much, she nearly spilled her tea. "Egyptian Collection, Beatrice Simpson speaking." Her myopic eyes widened and their gaze fell on Lauren.

Lauren could feel all the color leave her face. Bea didn't need to say anything. She knew who was on the line.

"I'm not sure, Mr. Fitzgerald. Just a moment." Pushing the hold button, she grimaced. "What do I tell him? He called your extension and no one answered. The museum operator told him to try me."

"Tell him I'm not here." Rising quickly, she placed the teacup on the desk. "And you won't be lying. I'm going to stop by my office and pick up some books. I'll work at home today."

Shaking her head, Bea pursed her lips. "Lauren, I think we should talk about this."

"What's to say? I've been a fool."

"Have you given him a chance to explain? He sounds pretty desperate."

"Not today, Bea, okay? I'm not ready for any advice." Lauren's eyes fell to the hold button, still blinking red. "Just tell him I'm not available."

Lauren couldn't think about Flynn or the break-ins any longer. There was work to do; files to be replaced, data to be processed. The pottery seminar was only days away. She had to begin putting normalcy back into her life, and her life was her work. That was all she needed for now.

The ever-present cup of tea beside her, Lauren sprawled on her couch, Dr. Jamieson's copy of *The Pictorial History of Etruscan Ceramics* resting on her lap. It was proving to be an excellent resource for the seminar. She had already taken several pages of notes.

The knock on the door was firm. Her first startled thought was that it was Flynn; somehow he'd gotten through the security door without buzzing. Lauren sat absolutely still, not daring to move. The knock came again, louder.

Checking the peephole, she saw that Officer Katherine O'Connell stood in the doorway. "Miss Michaels, may I come in?"

Lauren unlocked and opened the door, stepping away so the officer could enter. Then she closed the door and leaned back against it. "Is something wrong?"

"I guess not, now that I've seen you. When the report came up on the computer that it was your office that was vandalized at the Field Museum, I tried to call you. When I couldn't get any answer, I decided to stop by."

Lauren was surprised by the policewoman's concern for her and, guiltily, remembered her manners. "This is really very thoughtful of you. I had the phone unplugged. Please, sit down."

Shaking her head, Katherine O'Connell

smiled. "I've got to go. Just wanted you to know that we're still working on your attempted burglary. It's tough going, but we're trying."

After opening the door again, Lauren stopped the woman's retreat into the hallway. "Thank you for coming by . . . I do appreciate all you've done." It was an apology for her behavior on the night of the break-in.

Officer O'Connell met Lauren's eyes and nodded in acknowledgement. "You might give some thought to the two burglaries—on the outside chance that there is a connection."

Lauren was startled. Everyone else was trying to convince her these were random acts in a big city filled with violence. It was reassuring to realize that at least one other person thought there might be a link.

"If I think of anything, I have your number. Again, thanks for your concern."

Collapsing back onto the couch, Lauren was more determined than ever to discover what was going on. It was nice of Officer O'Connell to be considerate of her. But now it was time for her to stop avoiding the issue. She would/have to face it head on and see what she might find. As soon as she finished her notes on the pottery seminar, she would go back through every other book Dr. Jamieson had given her to see if somehow there was something unusual in one of them.

There was, but it seemed to have nothing to do with Operation Blackford.

On page two hundred and six of *The Pictorial History of Etruscan Ceramics*, scribbled in pencil in the margin, were some random hieroglyphics. A little alarm went off in her head. Dr. Jamieson had a scholar's abhorrence of writing in books. Could this have been written by someone else? Then she remembered this was the book that had been open on Dr. Jamieson's desk the night he died.

Staring back at her from the page were glossy colored photographs of round clay pots which had been used to hold cosmetics. These exact pots had been the source of their last debate about the link between Etruscan and Egyptian pottery. Vessels so similar to these had been discovered in the tombs of pharaohs that Dr. Jamieson had been convinced the Etruscan craft couldn't be a coincidence. The idealist in him had wanted to unite all the Mediterranean cultures through their artisans.

This couldn't really help her. She'd been right when she told Malcolm that Dr. Jamieson was probably working on a new argument for her to research. In his eagerness, and perhaps his weakness, for he had not been well that night, he'd scribbled his notes in the margin. But why in hieroglyphics? Something about it just wasn't right.

She traced his writing with her fingertip. Suddenly it seemed very important to discover what those hieroglyphics said. She was not very familiar with the symbols herself—it took years to truly master and manipulate the ancient glyphs—but she had the resources to decipher the writings.

The textbook on hieroglyphics wasn't on the table next to the phone. She must have left it in her office at the museum. On impulse, she plugged the phone back into the jack.

It rang immediately. It might be Bea, or even Officer O'Connell, she thought. She couldn't spend the rest of her life avoiding the phone because it might be *him*.

She answered it. Just as quickly, she slammed it back into its cradle.

She had made her point, Flynn decided. He wouldn't call her again, not until he discovered who the leak was. Then he could go to her and explain everything.

He picked up the phone again.

"I'd like to speak to the councilman. Tell him Flynn Fitzgerald is calling." His fingers tensed slightly as he considered how best to approach the arrogant and powerful councilman. "I'm going to stop in and see you, Councilman Blackford. It might be wise for your attorney to be present."

Geniality and friendliness oozed across the line from Blackford. Flynn grimaced.

"Two o'clock on Thursday would be fine."

Let Chuck and Malcolm work on the case from their points of view. Flynn was going to attack at the source. He had three days to figure out his strategy.

On Thursday, he knew exactly what he had to do. The office in City Hall was deceptively simple. Only a connoisseur would recognize the excess that had gone into the furnishings. A tall, angular woman with severely braided hair ushered him promptly into the inner sanctum.

Resting his hands on the mahogany desk for leverage, Blackford pushed his bulk out of the desk chair and strode forward. "Come in. Come in." He gestured toward a man seated to one side. "John and I have been speculating about your reasons for this little visit."

Flynn turned to the conservatively dressed man, one of the best defense attorneys money could buy. He knew of him by reputation only.

"John Denis. I've heard of your reputation. Glad you're here." Flynn smiled directly into the councilman's face as he continued pointedly, "Perhaps you can talk some sense into your client here."

The atmosphere turned instantly from geniality to frost. Mr. Denis folded his hands together and tapped two index fingers intermittently. As Councilman Blackford retreated behind his desk, Flynn and John Denis sized each other up. For now the battle was between them. Flynn saw a shrewd lawyer's poker face, older and more experienced than his own. Nothing would get to this man, he decided. Denis would be a man who played the angles, much like himself.

The only weakness in this room was sitting behind the highly polished walnut desk. Maybe, just maybe, he could scare the councilman into a slip.

The tapping fingers stopped. "What do you have in mind?" Denis asked.

"Just a thought. It must be difficult for your client to face this alone." Flynn paused long enough for the words to register. "The case is building. But it seems to me, some accommodation might be possible, if I could be pointed in the right direction."

Flynn glanced toward the desk. Councilman Blackford was running a maroon handkerchief over his forehead. That's it, squirm a little, Flynn thought. It never failed—give these crooks the slightest chance of saving themselves and they'd always jump.

"An interesting thought, Counselor." Mr. Denis unfolded his hands. "But not one we're prepared to consider at this point. Your evidence, such as it is . . ."

Flynn recognized that John Denis knew this was just a preliminary round. He wasn't going to linger here—he had one parting shot to deliver. "My evidence is growing. And from now on, there won't be any opportunities for further leaks from my office."

There was an audible gasp, followed by several dry coughs. "My asthma," Councilman Blackford muttered, once again raising the maroon handkerchief to his face.

Mr. Denis moved quickly to minimize his client's blunder. "You've given us something to think about." He said it smoothly, urging Flynn to the door at the same time.

Flynn wasn't sure how he ever made it back to his own office. The fishing expedition had paid off—but at what price?

Councilman Blackford's sputtering cough had been the tip-off. For weeks, Flynn had been avoiding the obvious—that the leak had to be someone inside, someone who knew as soon as he did what the next step in the case would be.

Looking back, he could see other cases where security breaches had eliminated a witness or protected a felon. But only with Operation Blackford had it become obvious that someone was trying to undermine his own credibility and ability. Flynn guessed the conspiracy involved more than one councilman, but the way things were going, he'd never get the chance to prove it. The D.A. and the mayor had already expressed their "concern."

Now he had a solid lead. Someone in his office was the leak. But he'd have to keep that knowledge to himself. He couldn't afford to tip anyone off.

As his mind raced through the long list of people who worked for him, he absent-mindedly capped and uncapped the fountain pen he had been given by the judge he had clerked for in his first year after law school. Much of the staff had been in place long before he came, and Betty, his secretary, had been with him since he first clerked. He knew these people, had socialized with them after work, knew their families. How could one of his own be involved?

Then he remembered Chuck's security report. It had been detailed and thorough. If it wasn't his office staff precisely, who else might have access to their papers? Cleaning and maintenance? Or maybe someone who came in before them and took the opportunity to rummage through his unlocked files or garbage.

He'd heard of a stockbroker's trash being used to get market tips. Maybe that was the leak. He jumped at the possibility. He wanted to be at ease with his colleagues again . . . so he could explain it all to Lauren.

The next day, the lake was so calm there wasn't a sailboat in sight. No wind in the Windy City today.

Flynn sat, as usual, with his back to the door. The memo, handwritten and nicely crumpled, was about halfway down inside his wastebasket. The trap was set.

Malcolm and Chuck found him staring

pensively into space when they burst into the office a few minutes later, followed by Taggart.

Tight-lipped, Flynn straightened in his chair, composed his face, and swung around. "What's going on now?" he asked calmly. He did feel calm. The situation was under control. If everything worked out, he'd have the leak plugged by Monday at the latest.

Taggart gave him a long, measured look. "I've got to talk to you. It's important."

The expression on Taggart's face brought Flynn to his feet. "Is it Lauren? Tell me!"

Taggart glanced at Malcolm and Chuck, clearly uncertain whether to proceed. He hesitated long enough for them to exchange bewildered stares. Then Malcolm made a move toward the door.

"No, Malcolm, sit down. You, too, Chuck. It's okay, Taggart."

The tension in the room was enormous as Malcolm and Chuck slid into the chairs facing Flynn's desk. The detective and the two men, Flynn's strongest supporters, were looking at Flynn as if he had lost his mind.

Never before had he felt the need to conceal his actions from anyone. But now he had had Lauren followed secretly and had set up a trap that he would have to keep to himself. He was in danger of losing his job and his reputation, of losing a case that he had spent months building. But somehow it had all lost its urgency. It almost seemed incidental. And this new vulnerability was the direct result of his feeling for Lauren. He would protect her above everybody else.

Flynn stood, outlined by the sunlit window behind him. "Well, Taggart?"

"Someone else is tailing Lauren Michaels." Taggart sat in a straight-backed wooden chair a little to one side of the desk.

"What?" Malcolm barked out the word.

"Someone else?" Chuck broke in. "Does that mean you have been tailing her, too?"

"On whose orders?" Malcolm demanded. His finger reached up to push his glasses back onto the bridge of his nose.

"Mine." Flynn's voice was quiet and controlled, oil on the troubled waters.

Malcolm relaxed back into his chair. "Then you did take my suggestion."

"Not really, Malcolm." Flynn carefully avoided looking at Taggart as he continued. "After someone tried to break into her apartment, I had Taggart keep an eye on her for her own protection. That's how I know she's not involved with Blackford."

"But Flynn, why?" Chuck was clearly still puzzled.

Lifting one brow, Flynn favored his friend with a wry smile. "And here I thought I was wearing it on my sleeve."

Malcolm nodded to himself, as if confirming a thought.

"I'm crazy about her and I don't want to

see anything happen to her." Flynn threaded his fingers through his hair and waited for a reaction.

"I can buy that." Chuck laughed.

"But what about the other tail?" Malcolm looked at Taggart.

"We haven't been able to get close enough to him to identify him. I'm here to suggest that we put double coverage on the girl, one to follow her and one to follow her tail. Maybe he'll lead us to something." Taggart spoke with the confidence of a professional.

"But if Lauren's not involved with Operation Blackford, why is someone else harassing her?" Malcolm pursued.

"Old trouble from her hometown. I know about it and it's no big deal, but I'd guess that's what this is all about." Flynn searched Taggart's deliberately blank face. "If you think a double tail will help, by all means, do it."

Chuck and Malcolm nodded in assent.

"About tonight . . ." Taggart began.

"Is Lauren home now?" Flynn cut in. At the answering nod, he continued, "Then she should be safe. Start the double tail tomorrow when she leaves her apartment."

Flynn recognized the look Taggart flashed him, assessing the situation, questioning why he had concealed the observation post from Malcolm and Chuck. It was bad enough that his concern forced him to invade her privacy like this, but he had to protect her! The only thing he could do to protect her privacy was to involve as few people as possible.

"Is there anything else, gentlemen? Okay, then. Monday morning we'll meet back here, discuss the results of the tail, and get on with your reports on Operation Blackford."

Flynn dismissed them, and with them his thoughts of Blackford and the leak.

Lauren was another matter. He just couldn't deal with her. And until his other problem was solved, he didn't think she would trust him. So he was doing the best he could under the circumstances. The more he thought of it, the more he decided that anything that concerned her should be kept strictly between himself and Taggart. If they could track down her other tail, they could put a stop to the harassment. Then maybe she'd be willing to listen to him.

9 Flynn's hands gripped the steering wheel. What was the matter with him? He'd never pursued where he wasn't wanted before. He wasn't a kid to wear his heart on his sleeve. But she wasn't a kid either.

All the way to her apartment, Flynn tried to convince himself that he was just going to drive by. He didn't have a prayer—he pulled up and parked.

Lauren paced. She couldn't walk at night in the city, so she paced a neat square in her small apartment. It would get monotonous, and it might take all night, but she was going to keep walking until she got it out of her system. It? Who was she kidding? Him.

How could she have been so deceived? After all that had happened, hadn't she learned anything? She had believed in Flynn because of Dr. Jamieson. Wouldn't he have been surprised to find out his hero had feet of clay?

She looked around her apartment. Memories of Flynn crowded at her. He had been wonderful to her after the robbery. He'd cleaned up the mess and stayed to make her feel safe. He'd kissed her. . . .

She abruptly stopped in her pattern and turned on the radio for distraction. She really couldn't keep thinking about him. The song's words filtered into her thoughts. If there was anything she didn't need, it was some singer telling her that "love would conquer all." She flipped the radio back off.

If she continued trying to decipher the hieroglyphics Dr. Jamieson had penciled into *The Pictorial History of Etruscan Ceramics*, surely she could put Flynn out of her mind.

She spread the book out on the kitchen table, along with several references she had brought from the museum, and tracing paper. Egyptian hieroglyphic writing was a logosyllabic system, she reminded herself. Of the seven hundred signs, the majority represented words. Only about one hundred of the signs could also be syllables. She studied the glyphs in front of her; they weren't the ones used for syllables. If that had been Dr. Jamieson's code, she'd never figure the message out, because each syllable only coded the consonant sound. It would take until Christmas to plug in all the variations of vowels. No, the marks in the books were pictographs, vaguely familiar to her. She figured if she traced them and played with each picture separately, it might jog her memory. In a writing system as advanced as the Egyptians', the glyph stood for that picture and all the ideas that were normally associated with it. She had symbols of ancient Egyptian culture—the crook, the game board, the dung beetle, the serpent, the ankh. She traced precisely and filled in the dark shapes with her pencil. She rearranged their order—horizontally, vertically. Why couldn't she figure this out? Dr. Jamieson, smart as he had been, was not a hieroglyphic expert. She must be missing the point.

Finally, she pushed her hair behind her ears in disgust. This was getting her nowhere fast. Maybe if she . . .

The phone rang, breaking her concentration. She picked it up distractedly.

"Hello."

"Lauren, this is Flynn. I'm downstairs and we need to talk. Please buzz me through."

The phone nearly fell out of her grasp, but her other hand automatically supported her grip.

"Leave me alone."

"We've got to talk." Where was the cool, articulate self-possessed lawyer now? "I can explain, if you'll only listen."

"I'm not interested in anything you have to say." She put the receiver down firmly to punctuate her words, gripped by an almost physical pain.

* * *

This was his last chance. After tomorrow, she'd have too much protection. And they all thought Lauren's problems didn't have anything to do with Operation Blackford. Lucky for him! The only thing he hadn't gotten a good look at was her bedroom. He'd start there.

Carefully, he pulled the black ski mask down over his face. Then he slid open the glass door and stepped out onto the balcony. He swung the rope up, catching it so he could swing over to reach her bedroom.

Noiselessly, he landed in the middle of the adjoining balcony. For a moment he stood listening, then he checked the street below. No familiar cars. He reached into his pocket and drew out a long, slim knife.

"Who's there?" Taggart's gravelly voice called from behind the door.

"Flynn."

"What the h . . ." Taggart opened it to find Flynn standing in the corridor. "Geez, you look terrible. Bad day at the office?"

Flynn pushed past Taggart into the room. The curtains were open, and a telescope stood in position next to a hard wooden desk chair, aimed at Lauren's apartment across the street. A low lamp burned in one corner, magazines stacked on the table underneath it.

"Anything going on over there?"

"Nothing I can see. This stakeout has really been a waste of time." Taggart scratched his head and stretched. "You make up your mind about that girl yet?"

"Of course I have." Flynn gestured impatiently. "You were in the office this afternoon, you heard what I said."

"Yeah. Something's bothering me about that."

Flynn sat on the edge of the bed. "Okay. Shoot."

"It seemed like you didn't want Malcolm and Chuck to know about this stakeout. Why?"

"The fewer people that know we're watching her, the better. She's not a criminal. I feel like I'm invading her privacy. I don't see any reason to get others involved."

"So?"

"For some reason, I feel she needs my protection." He stood impatiently. "Damn it, Taggart, that girl is special. . . . I'm not going to let anything happen to her." He pushed his fingers back through his salt-and-pepper hair. "Even though it's got nothing to do with Blackford, something's going on with her."

"Sure," Taggart soothed. "Well, nothing's going on tonight."

"If you're bored here, I'll take over," Flynn snapped.

"I would like to grab some fresh coffee." Taggart reached for his coat. "Be back in a half hour."

"Take your time."

Flynn pulled the curtain away from the window and surveyed the view. The panes had been freshly washed, inside and out, to improve visibility. He glanced quickly at Lauren's window before turning away, disgusted with himself. Is this what he had come to: spying on the woman he loved?

Her curtains had been drawn, but the light behind them indicated she was still up. Had she closed them because she knew she was being watched? He paced in fury.

He stopped in front of the window again, overwhelmed by his desire to see her, then turned away once more.

He sat wearily in the chair and considered his options. If only she still believed in him, he could be with her now. They could figure this out together. Maybe someone from her life in Indiana had surfaced to harass her. He'd have Taggart check into that theory tomorrow. Maybe her stepfather was trying to pay her back from prison. What else could it be?

He knew Bernard Jamieson was too trustworthy to have said something out of turn to Lauren. He reconsidered the plan he had devised to catch the leak. It seemed pretty airtight to him. He hadn't even told Malcolm and Chuck, to protect them in case the whole thing blew up in his face. No reason for them all to lose their jobs.

It had been about fifteen minutes since he'd taken his last look. This time he focused on the glass on her window. The light

was still on and he couldn't sense any
movement.

He swung the telescope slightly to the
right. There she was, sitting at the kitchen
window, right where they'd shared breakfast. She was hunched over, concentrating.
The lens picked up and enlarged the
slightest detail, her lip caught in determination, the slight frown that told him she
was working on a problem.

He watched, fascinated, in spite of himself. She was lovely sitting in the reflected
kitchen light. Lovely and vulnerable.

Some instinct made him slowly pan the
telescope back to the left, past the curtained living room window, to the darkened
balcony outside her bedroom. He refocused
the lens.

Nothing.

He sank back into the chair. Apprehen-
sion was making him jumpy. Lauren was
right there in her kitchen. She was fine.
Nothing could happen to her.

Where the hell was Taggart? He should
leave, get a good night's sleep. It wasn't doing any good sitting here, watching her. Tomorrow he would confront her at the
museum. He had to get this rift between
them resolved so he could concentrate on
Operation Blackford. The councilman
wasn't going to like having to deal with an
offer of immunity—even explaining it to his
friends. Flynn was certain the fur would

start to fly as soon as that rumor got around.

He couldn't resist one last look.

A black-clad figure swung from the balcony next to Lauren's and landed softly outside her bedroom window. Flynn watched him try the French door. It was secure. That wouldn't be enough to stop him, though. In growing horror, he watched the intruder pull out a switchblade to jimmy the lock.

Glancing down again at the street below, he checked for cars. None. Good. This was his last chance. If Lauren Michaels had anything in that apartment, he had to get it now. If not ... well, he would just have to shut her up for good. He couldn't take the chance that she might stumble onto anything. Especially now that Flynn had taken such an interest in her. Even if Flynn already knew something, without Lauren there would be no proof.

Inside, he heard the phone ringing. He took advantage of the noise to carefully insert the knife into the crack of the doorway. A moment later he inched the glass doors apart.

Flynn grabbed the phone and dialed her number, then swung the scope to watch her shadow cross the living room.

He put the lens back on her balcony just as she answered.

"Lauren, it's Flynn. Don't hang up! Get

out of your apartment. There's a guy trying
to get into your bedroom."

"Where are you? And why are you trying to frighten me with these ridiculous stories?" Her voice was trembling.

"Believe me. I'm watching him through
a telescope . . . Damn! He's got the door
open—Lauren, get out of there now!"

*The bedroom was dark. Reaching for his
pencil flashlight, he tiptoed across the room.
He'd start with the chest of drawers. He began to open the first drawer, when Lauren's
voice, loud and hysterical, followed by the
phone slamming down, froze him into position.*

*Quickly, he crouched behind the bed-
room door. He wouldn't let anyone stop him
now, no matter what the cost.*

What could he do? Forgetting the phone,
the telescope, Flynn had only one thought.
He had to get over there. He had to save
her.

He ran out into the hallway and punched
the elevator button. Too slow. He'd never
get to her in time. He spotted an exit sign:
a stairwell. Only two flights, that would be
faster than waiting for the elevator in this
old building. Frantically, he raced down the
stairs, his heels pounding.

He made it out into the street. Gulping
deep breaths of fresh air, he charged into
the traffic. Horns blared. There was no time

to look up at her window. It wouldn't have done him any good, nothing could be seen from the street anyway. He vaulted over the divider, hoping desperately she'd believed him and left the apartment.

How long had it been? His breath came in a series of shallow pants. Brakes squealed as a car skidded to a halt inches from him. The driver leaned out the window and yelled something obscene, but Flynn kept running.

Be safe, he prayed silently.

He slammed through the revolving door. There was no tenant conveniently there to let him in this time. He rammed the security door in despair.

"Shit!"

He hit every call button, while trying to dial her number. There was no answer. His mind raced frantically. He had to get inside.

He had to get to Lauren somehow.

Then he noticed an old-fashioned fire alarm high on the wall. He broke the glass with his fist, a thin line of blood trickling to his wrist, and pulled the lever down. Damn! Was it broken? There was no alarm. Suddenly, an overweight man in a custodian's uniform with a large ring of keys on his belt appeared from the side hall and stood staring at him through the glass.

"Let me in! I'm with the State Attorney's Office!" Flashing his credentials, Flynn slammed his palm against the pane, leaving a smear of blood.

As if in slow motion, the janitor opened the door. "What d'ya think . . . Hey, come back here!"

He was in; he was close. He had to be on time. He jabbed at the elevator buttons. Again he noticed a stairwell. But four flights up would take too long.

"I'm callin' the police!" the custodian bellowed.

Flynn glanced around. "Do that! And hurry!"

The elevator took forever to descend. He couldn't wait any longer. He started for the stairwell, but heard the elevator door open behind him. He whirled to enter.

She was there.

"Lauren, thank God you're all right!" He felt like a stranger to himself, experiencing emotions he never knew existed. In the last few minutes he thought he'd aged ten years, but now he felt like a kid again, so full of joy it was bursting out of him.

He reached for her but stopped short of touching her, remembering her anger on the phone.

She was so pale. And she was trembling.

"You were right," she said in wonder, her eyes wide and frightened. "Right after I hung up the phone I heard noises in my bedroom. I ran into the hallway, but he didn't follow me. The elevator came and I started down. How did you get here so fast?"

"It doesn't matter now. You stay right here! I'm going to get this guy." Flynn stepped toward the elevator.

"No, Flynn. Don't go up there!" She put a pleading hand on his arm. "Stay with me. Please!" Falling heavily against him, Lauren wound both arms around his waist. "Please don't go!"

His delight that she trusted him again, that she was willing to touch him, that she might be worried about his safety, was tempered by the urgency of finding out who was trying to hurt her. "Lauren, it's all right now." His voice sounded nearly normal to him, but he realized he was holding her in a grip which numbed his hands. "You've got to let me get this guy. It could solve everything."

Two police arrived, and a firetruck's screaming siren could be heard approaching. Officer O'Connell and her partner came around the corner. "What's the trouble here, Mr. Fitzgerald?"

For several seconds Lauren stared up at him in silence, then she grinned feebly before trying to step out of his arms. But he refused to let her move from his side.

"It isn't a fire, although I pulled the alarm. There's another intruder in Lauren's apartment."

"You take the stairs," Office O'Connell

told her partner. Without further hesitation she took the elevator.

Flynn pressed his lips quickly to Lauren's forehead. "I've got to go with them. I can help."

"Not without me, you're not," she muttered, following him into the second elevator, which had just arrived.

By the time they reached the fourth floor, the intruder was long gone. There was no evidence of a break-in, except the broken lock on her patio door. The apartment hadn't been searched or trashed like before. Only one thing was missing—a page of Dr. Jamieson's book had been ripped out; the page with the hieroglyphics. All of her tracings were gone, too.

"Why would a thief want that?" Lauren was confused. "*I* couldn't even figure out what they meant."

"Can you recreate them?" Officer O'Connell asked once Lauren had explained what was stolen.

"Sure." Lauren sat at the table and drew the Egyptian symbols. "These are the ones I was working on. In this order they don't quite make sense, but they're familiar."

"Can I have this?"

Lauren nodded. "I'm not going to forget them now."

"Let us know if you decode them. It might be a clue." The policewoman smiled kindly. "I think you'll be okay here. Not many people will try to come in over the balcony. But be careful.''

"She won't be here, Officer." Flynn looked at Lauren tenderly. "I'm going to take her somewhere safe."

Lauren allowed that remark to pass; she didn't have the strength or the desire to argue with him now.

Officer O'Connell assured them that she would call for an extra squad car to patrol the neighborhood through the night.

Flynn jury-rigged her balcony door shut while she checked through everything one more time. Nothing else was missing. He watched her gather all the reference books and papers and stack them in a neat pile.

"You will come with me, won't you?" he asked.

"Flynn, I . . ."

For three long breaths they stood, staring at one another.

Flynn sighed deeply, stepping forward to place his hands carefully on her shoulders. She did not flinch.

"You've got to forgive me. Everything I've done has been to protect you. And I'm going to keep protecting you until we figure this out." He lifted one hand to her cheek. "Together."

More than anything in this world, she wanted to believe him. Her indecision must have shown on her face, for Flynn took her hand and led her to the couch.

"Lauren, listen to me. This whole thing

has turned into a nightmare. But I have a plan to trap whoever it is in my office who's leaking to Blackford. Now all I have to worry about is you."

Lifting both her hands, he held them tightly between his own. "What I'm trying to tell you is that I know you're not involved. I trust you. But I have to protect you from whoever is trying to hurt you." His shoulders sagged, but his eyes, brilliant with emotion, never left her face. "I was terrified when I saw that guy on your balcony. I've never felt so helpless before. Please, you must let me watch over you."

He waited nervously for her to answer.

Lauren couldn't think of anything to say. The right words—and they had to be right— wouldn't seem to form in her brain. Then she noticed his hand for the first time, the knuckles scraped raw and spotted with dried blood.

"What happened to your hand, Flynn?"

"It's nothing. I did it when I broke the fire alarm."

"But you hurt yourself!" she gasped, surprised at how much she wanted to soothe away that pain.

He shrugged. "I couldn't think of any other way to get in."

All of a sudden, she knew what she wanted. Now, seeing the lengths to which he would go to protect her, she could believe in him. The only barrier between them was her pride.

Slowly, she untangled her hands from his and raised his knuckles to her lips, pressing soft kisses against the roughened skin. "You really mean what you're saying, don't you, Flynn? Where do you want to take me?"

"Home. I'm taking you home with me."

10 Flynn's brownstone on Astor, in the exclusive Gold Coast section of Chicago's famed near Northside, was beautifully restored. Polished wood floors, crystal chandeliers, and the dark carved wooden staircase gleamed in the light from the foyer. It was an exquisite house, but nearly empty of furniture. What little there was was nondescript at best. Lauren shuddered and looked at Flynn in surprise.

Flynn only laughed when he saw her reaction to the 1950s bachelor-style furnishings. "Would you believe the good stuff's out being recovered?" he joked. "Really, I've put so much into the restoration, I haven't gotten around to the furniture. Maybe you could give me some much needed help."

"I'd love to." Lauren smiled easily at his enthusiasm. Dear Dr. Jamieson, you were right after all about your Fitzgerald.

He took her hand. "Come into the study. That at least is furnished and ready for company."

He lit the gas fire in the grate as she wandered around the room. Obviously, here was where he lived. Floor-to-ceiling bookcases crammed with law and reference books covered every wall. In front of a mullioned window stood one of the largest rolltop desks she'd ever seen. It was of beautiful polished oak, piled high with papers, every nook and cranny filled. Spread open on top of the mess was a paperback science fiction novel. There was a crewel wing chair and footstool to the left of the stone fireplace, and a brass lamp burned on the gate-legged table beside it. Across from the chair, a well worn cream leather couch beckoned comfortably. She sank into it, enjoying the warmth from the small fire.

A loud quacking noise filled the silence. Startled, Lauren sat up and looked around.

Flynn lifted off the top of a duck decoy. "Taggart! Yes, we're inside safely. . . . You get anything? . . . All right, then. See you Monday."

Lauren laughed nervously. "That's a pretty funny phone ring."

Flynn nodded and dialed a number. "A birthday present from Malcolm and Chuck. . . . No more calls tonight. I'll get my messages in the morning." He turned back to her. "Would you like something to drink? How about some brandy?"

Behind the couch, set into the bookcase, was a small bar. Flynn lifted out two crystal brandy snifters and poured a small amount of Courvoisier into each. Reaching from behind her, he practically set the glass in her lap.

His nearness enveloped her, the scent of him tugging at her senses. His hand gently caressed her cheek before he withdrew his arm and moved to sit in the wing chair.

Sipping slowly at the fiery liquid, she allowed it to soothe her quaking insides. She was here, alone with Flynn in his home, and she was so tense and nervous she had to force herself to sit quietly.

Flynn cradled his glass in his long-fingered hands, heating the brandy with their warmth before lifting it to his lips. Over the rim of the snifter, he watched her watching him. Awareness filtered into the cozy room, awareness and something else, a feeling, an intensity of emotion which had been constantly changing and growing between them.

Here she was at last. In his study, in his home, where he'd imagined her. She wore a University of Indiana sweatshirt and faded jeans, her makeup was worn off, her face flushed, and her hair tangled. But she was as beautiful to him as on the night of the banquet. Could that have been only last weekend?

He'd imagined love would be a consuming flame within him. But now that she was here, love was a low ember smoldering steadily, waiting for her to fan the flame to life.

She sipped again, and they began to talk at the same moment.

"What do . . ."

"I'm not . . ."

Their smiles were in gentle understanding.

"I'm not sure what's going on," she continued. "I can't imagine that my stepfather or any of his associates would want to harass me. That just doesn't seem right." She didn't really want to talk about, or even think about all the facts she had spent the week sorting out. Dr. Jamieson and the hieroglyphics were jumbled in her mind with the feelings she was experiencing now.

"I don't have any other explanation." He reached a hand toward her. "But I can promise you, I'll find out who's doing this and why."

His hand was an invitation to comfort, to security, to a new beginning.

His suit coat had been discarded, his tie loosened. His hair was mussed from being habitually raked off his forehead. Deep worry lines creased his face, and dark shadows beneath his eyes dimmed their luster. But to Lauren, none of that mattered.

She reached across to touch him. "Thank you, Flynn. I know I've said that before. But I really do feel safe here with you. And . . ' I'm sorry for doubting you."

Slowly, he stood and pulled her up and into his arms, the dancing flames casting shadows across the planes of his face.

"I'm glad you understand. There's no reason you should ever trust a lawyer again after what happened to you in Indiana," he said softly, one finger carefully stroking her hair. His knuckle brushed her cheek.

"Let's not talk about that anymore," she murmured.

He took the brandy snifter from her hand and put it, along with his, on the mantle. Suddenly they were staring into each other's faces, making silent promises.

"Lauren . . ." His lips moved lingeringly from her mouth to her earlobe, and she could feel him, just for a moment, bury his head in her hair.

His hand reached out to caress her cheek, giving her the courage to lift her lips for another kiss. The softness and warmth of his mouth against hers stirred yearnings within her. He had kissed her before, but this time seemed to be fulfilling a promise.

She felt he was reaching right through to her soul, shattering all the barriers she had tried to erect. Her heart pounded in her ears as a burning desire to touch him, have him kiss her again, slowly consumed her.

He watched her eyes widen and darken with passion, passion that he had evoked. The flame in him burst into life. She involuntarily pressed against him and he groaned.

Lauren's body was aflame, every nerve tingling, for at this moment, the attraction between them was so powerful it left her breathless with anticipation and fear. That fear crept into her eyes, and suddenly he retreated, pushing her gently back, but holding onto her as if he couldn't bear to let her go.

"You're so beautiful," he murmured. "Sit with me a while by the fire."

He pulled some pillows off the couch and made a nest for them on the floor. Then he drew her down to sit between his legs, and clasped his arms around her shoulders.

"There's something comforting about a fire." His breath stirred her hair. His gentleness surprised her, his patience and understanding made her eager.

She snuggled back into his embrace and brought one of his hands up to study it: long, lean fingers, lightly furred, hard knuckles; calloused palms. She kissed the hand tentatively—the hand he had hurt trying to protect her—and grew bolder as she felt him stir. Her tongue licked the joint between thumb and forefinger.

His other hand pressed just above her heart, holding her tightly to him. She took his middle finger into her mouth, gently sucking.

Suddenly, unexpectedly, she was pulled around to face him. Laying across his lap, she stared at him, wordlessly exploring the longing he evoked, attempting to understand his need, and her own.

And she reached up to touch him at the exact moment he leaned down to her.

Lauren moaned into his mouth as his tongue invaded knowingly, and her hands tangled in the curls at his nape, forcing him closer.

She had never felt so cherished, so desirable.

He became utterly still, although she could feel how he struggled for breath. His arms tightened around her for an instant and then relaxed. Only heartbeats separated them. "I think I'll show you the guest room now."

She couldn't let this go—these feelings.

"Flynn?" His name was the question she couldn't bring herself to ask.

Something lit the depths of his blue eyes. Whispering softly, words she couldn't quite understand, he pressed his palms against the skin of her back, under her sweatshirt.

"Yes," she breathed, encouraging him, encouraging herself. The dancing flames were in his eyes now as he unclasped her bra and lifted her shirt away.

"My God, you're so beautiful," he groaned, reaching out to cup her breasts with his long fingers. Excitement and pure pleasure pierced her when he sought one hardened nipple and sucked on it gently. Arching toward him, her head flung back, she moaned as he moved from peak to peak, sucking and kissing.

Her fingers struggled with his shirt buttons. Finally she had them all open. She levered away from him, desiring to show him the passion he had awakened in her. She drew her nails over his hard chest, puckering the nipples, teasing them. Her hands massaged his shoulders then tailed down his arms.

He lay still for a short time, then his hand went questioningly to her belt buckle. Her answer was to reach for his. Together they slid out of unwanted clothes. He pressed her back into the soft carpet, the fire outlining the pronounced curve of his back. Suddenly there was nothing between them. There was only the heat of his body and the need to be even closer, which drove her to press into him, her hands stroking his rippling muscles.

With infinite tenderness he kissed and licked at her small fine breasts. Then he lowered his head to her taut stomach, tonguing her navel.

Soft whimpers of desire escaped her. "Flynn . . . oh, Flynn . . ."

He gazed up into her face, urgent with need. She caressed his cheek tenderly. When once again he moved down on her body, she urged him, opening herself eagerly to the touch of his fingers and tongue.

Pleasure built upon pleasure as Flynn led her through a blaze of delight. The world contained nothing but them and this piercing sweet rapture they shared.

They came together in a vortex of passion, and he soothed her, raining gentle kisses over her face and tucking her chin down onto his shoulder, stroking her back until she slept.

Lauren stirred in her sleep. The dream of contentment, fulfillment had shifted. A serpent sprang out of a reed basket and coiled around a dung beetle. She recognized the ancient symbol of evil and recoiled. Her body came up against something solid—she couldn't get away. . . .

She opened her eyes, surprised to find herself on the floor. Warmth from the fire and Flynn had allowed her to sleep. Now, a nagging doubt had wakened her.

Flynn's arm was curled protectively around her and kept her secure against his muscled warmth. Carefully, she turned to study his face, still in the haven of his arm. It was shadowed in the flickering firelight. She remembered drowning in the intense blue of his eyes during the precious moments of the night, as he had covered her and made them one. She knew she had found everything, especially security, here with him.

What had awakened her, then?

Something disturbed her. Some detail she'd forgotten in the excitement and joy of discovering Flynn. The serpent! That was it. The serpent in her dream had wakened her. Somehow she knew it didn't belong with the other hieroglyphics that Dr. Jamieson had written in the margin of his book.

Carefully, she extracted herself from his

embrace. Away from his body heat, she shivered and reached for his shirt to cover herself. She placed her own oversized sweatshirt on him in return.

Quietly, trying not to disturb him, she moved behind the desk and switched the interior light on. It's tiny beam barely illuminated the desk's surface. She searched through the piles of paper for a blank sheet.

Concentrating, she remembered all the symbols and drew them on the page. They weren't in the order Dr. Jamieson had written them, but they were all there: the amun—the game board; the ankh—symbol of life; the crook—royal symbol of authority. Subconsciously she had started a new column for the kheperu—the dung beetle, symbol of manifestation; and the neb—the reed basket that signified lord. The only symbol that didn't seem to fit was the serpent. She had written it at the bottom of the page.

Several glyphs represented the serpent. Most of them were good. In fact, Egyptian women often wore bracelets or amulets in the shape of a snake to protect their households or themselves. The coiled serpent, the uraeus, was symbolic of royal wisdom, she knew. That would have fit in better with these other symbols. Even the serpent holding its tail in its mouth—symbolizing immortality—would have fit in with these other glyphs.

But the snake Dr. Jamieson had drawn

was the negative symbol. It stood for darkness and death.

Had he been trying to tell her something about his own death? Had he felt the last attack coming?

The first symbols were familiar, and she had written them in an order she knew was correct. All she would have to do was figure it out.

Idly doodling, she re-copied the symbols in the order Dr. Jamieson had written them down in the margin of the page. Nothing.

Her feet were getting cold and she wanted to go back to the fire, to Flynn. But she felt compelled to work on the puzzle. She stretched and yawned. Her pencil inadvertently drew a line between the two columns of figures.

Casually, she elongated the mark, curving it into an oval border. That was right! She enclosed the other side quickly, excitement hurrying her fingers. Yes, this was right!

She had formed a double cartouche—the royal signature. This was for one of the most famous pharaohs of all time: the boy king, Tutankhamen.

"That's it!" she exclaimed aloud, wondering how she could have missed it before. The glyphs all belonged in the double cartouche of King Tut's name Amun-Tut-Ankh—"the living image of Amun," and Mebkheprure—"the lord of manifestations is Ra.'' How could something so simple, so obvious have escaped her for so long?

But this solution didn't really answer any questions, just raised more. Why would Dr. Jamieson have written these symbols out of order in his book? They didn't have anything to do with Etruscan pottery. And why would he, with his brilliant memory, have forgotten so many of the proper glyphs to complete the cartouches, and included an evil snake instead?

She'd been so intent on her discovery that the hand brushing her shoulder startled her. She shrieked.

''Flynn!''

''Sweetheart, sorry I frightened you.'' He pointed to the paper. ''What's this?''

''I've solved the hieroglyphics Dr. Jamieson wrote. It doesn't make sense, though. They're just King Tutankhamen's signature.''

His fingers caressed the back of her neck. ''You're freezing.''

''I'm all right. I don't think this can be very important, though. I wonder why the thief took it?''

He swiveled the chair around and pulled her upright. Then she realized for the first time that he was gloriously naked. *''You* must be freezing,'' she chuckled.

''Far from it,'' he muttered, his glance caressing the curve of one breast revealed by his open shirt and traveling down to her thighs. "I don't think I've ever seen one of my shirts look better."

"Flynn, I think we should call Officer O'Connell. She wanted to know what those glyphs meant."

"Not right now." He hauled her into his arms. "You said yourself they can't be important." He smiled and passion darkened his eyes. "I can think of something much more important."

Flynn swept Lauren into his arms and carried her slowly up the thickly carpeted stairs. This was where she belonged, it felt so right. It was right.

Her head fell back against his shoulder and his lips caressed the length of her throat, nibbling, kissing, taking her earlobe between his teeth, and an instant later licking away the light tingle of pain.

Lauren felt as if he were knotting her insides with silken cords of sensual pleasure winding tighter and tighter as they climbed each step. Her hands tangled in his hair. Tenderness floated in the air between them, whispers not precisely understood but felt deep inside her.

Flynn pushed open the bedroom door and, moving quickly, laid her gently on the bed.

Lauren trembled in anticipation as their eyes locked and held. No one had ever looked at her like this, with such tenderness and need. Please, please, Flynn, see the same emotions in my eyes, she wished silently, reaching her arms out to him.

He lowered his body onto hers, pressing her deeper into the softness. Her need to be even closer to him deepened to an ache. Finally, when Lauren thought she could be wound no tighter, his lips slowly descended to taste her mouth.

Then his fingers caught the shirt, spreading it slowly over the rise of her breasts and smooth flatness of her stomach.

Nuzzling his face into her belly, he said her name once in a whisper, his breath feathering over her skin. Slowly he trailed perfect kisses in the hollows and curves of her body. She felt he was worshipping her with his every touch.

Lauren drew shuddering, gasping breaths, her insides growing tighter and tighter beneath the exquisite pressure of his exploration, her legs trembling as his tongue caressed the satin of her inner thighs.

"Flynn . . . I . . ." Sliding over her, he stopped her words with a burning kiss.

Need for him rioted in her veins, nearly driving her wild when he took one nipple deeply into his mouth, his knee pressing urgently between her thighs.

Her body moved restlessly beneath him, soft whimpers stirring his hair as she buried her face in it, her hands desperately clutching his shoulders.

Suddenly lifting his head, his eyes wide

and dark, Flynn caught her face in his palms.

"You're so perfect, love," he whispered against her trembling lips. "Perfect for me. . . ."

"You're perfect, Flynn. . . ." she groaned, the fever consuming her so that now it was she who rained kisses down his chest, and it was she who felt him tremble as her lips caressed the strong muscles of his inner thighs and beyond, filling herself with the taste of him.

"Lauren . . . love . . ." His hands lifted her urgently.

"Yes . . . love me . . . now. . . ." she urged.

As he entered her slowly, and then more fully, the coil wound tighter and tighter. Each movement of his body was a caress to her senses, each word of delight he whispered a joy, until the pleasure could be held no longer and the coil snapped, enveloping them in exotic warmth.

They were both caught fast in the torrent, clinging to one another and the rapture which carried them with it.

11

Lauren woke to a blaze of sunlight and the warmth of Flynn's body alongside hers. He was watching her sleep, his eyes wide, soft, and penetrable, every muscle and line of his body relaxed, warm, and still. His arm tightened around her, and Lauren nestled her cheek deeper into the hollow of his shoulder, preparing to fall back into dreams. He smelled male—early morning, oh-so-right, Flynn! She sighed in contentment.

Finding her chin with his fingers, he tilted her face upward toward his. In the bright sunlight of early morning he looked younger, happier, contented also. His salt-and-pepper hair rioted in a halo of color.

"You're something else, sweet," he whispered, his voice a deep caress.

Complimented, she snuggled against him, her breasts pressing into the soft curls on his chest. She was content to lie peacefully in his arms while his palm stroked her hair to her shoulder, then played a light staccato down her arm to her fingertips. He lifted her hand to his lips, nibbling gently at her knuckles.

"Such clever little hands." Taking one finger into his mouth, he sucked on it gently, much as she had the night before. "And what do you want to do with the rest of the day?" he asked in amusement. His brilliant eyes deepened to sapphire and widened in desire.

A hot rush of demanding excitement compelled her to cover one breast with his strong hand and arch up to meet his mouth with her own parted lips.

Lauren woke again to strong afternoon sunlight streaming in through the window blinds, which were off-white, bold, and clean. The furniture was all straight sparse lines, but a Burberry carpet and Ralph Lauren crimson-and-cream plaid sheets and spread gave the room warmth and color.

Quickly slipping into a robe spread across a chair, she padded downstairs.

She felt a change in herself, a lightness; the buoyant joy of someone with no worries, no doubts. It was right to be here in Flynn's house, in Flynn's life. He made her feel complete, she really couldn't describe it in any other terms. All of yesterday was gone—the doubts, the uncertainties, the disappointments. Being with Flynn more than made up for the deficiencies of her former life. Feeling as though she had been given another beginning, she wanted nothing more than to go into Flynn's arms.

He was in the kitchen. Rested and showered, his hair neatly combed, he wore a blue open-necked shirt and jeans that hugged his narrow hips. He was barefoot.

His gaze swung quickly to her. "You're up! I was going to bring you breakfast in bed."

"I'll run back upstairs, if you like," she teased. "But it's a little past breakfast time, don't you think?"

She wandered farther into the room, standing on tiptoes to peer over his shoulder. "What are you making?"

He gave her a smile which went straight to her heart. "I couldn't give you just anything. It's eggs Fitzgerald."

"Is that anything like eggs Benedict?" she asked, pressing an open kiss at the nape of his neck where his hair curled slightly. She could feel his heartbeat quicken beneath her palms where they pressed against his chest.

"I hope so!" His voice was suddenly filled with laughter. "Let's try it. I've got big plans for today."

Breakfast was surprisingly delicious. Sectioned grapefruit, oversized blueberry muffins, and the eggs Fitzgerald—which she discovered meant cheese sauce instead of Hollandaise.

"That old college job at the sorority," he

laughed when she complimented his cooking.

After they had eaten and finished their second cup of tea, he shooed her upstairs for a shower. "You have twenty minutes, tops! I've got things to do, people to see."

The "people" were the orangutans at Lincoln Park Zoo. Flynn was outrageous, chatting to them as if they were old friends, introducing each one to Lauren individually. Chicago's weather, for once, cooperated. The zoo was full of young families, babies in strollers and children tugging indulgent parents excitedly to the next exhibit. Lauren secretly longed to be one of them.

Flynn's fingers tightened around her hand almost as if he'd read her thoughts. It was a day to forget their troubles and delight in each other's company.

"Let's go!" He pulled her away from the big cats. "I'm ready for the beach."

They crossed the bicycle path, jammed with riders, dodged serious joggers engrossed in their headsets, and stopped to watch a softball game in progress. He'd made some sandwiches, but they weren't hungry, so they sat at the water's edge throwing crumbs to the gulls, coaxing them closer.

All of that magical day she was at Flynn's side; his arm was constantly draped around her shoulders, or his hand held hers. Now they sat close together, thighs touching, and every once in a while when their eyes met, they couldn't keep from kissing. All of Lauren's nightmares slowly began to dissolve in a haze of happiness.

Late in the afternoon, Flynn jogged over to a concession stand because Lauren was consumed with a sudden craving for popcorn. She sat on a shaded park bench weaving idyllic dreams of happiness. A hand touched her shoulder lightly and she turned to find Malcolm standing behind her. "Hello, Lauren."

Surprised, she twisted around and rose quickly to her feet. "Hi, Malcolm. What are you doing here? You just missed Flynn. He'll be right back."

His brown eyes, magnified by thick glass lenses, stared solemnly at her. Self-consciously, she tugged at the hem of her sweatshirt, suddenly wishing she had gone with Flynn to get the popcorn.

"You and Flynn are getting to be good friends, aren't you? Just like you and Uncle Bernard." Pushing his glasses higher on his nose, Malcolm stepped closer to her.

She unconsciously retreated a step, then realized it and stopped herself. This was Malcolm, Flynn's friend. "Your uncle was very dear to me," she said softly. But the lighthearted mood of the day fled abruptly. Malcolm's presence had reminded her of all the problems she and Flynn still had to solve.

"Yes, he was . . . special," Malcolm continued. His mouth curved slightly in what, for him, constituted a smile. "Here's Flynn now. Looks like he's eaten half your popcorn."

"Hey, Malcolm! Getting your two miles in today? Kind of late, aren't you?" Flynn's face was flushed, and that unruly curl had fallen onto his forehead. Handing Lauren the half-empty bag of popcorn, he casually flung an arm around her shoulders. "Lauren and I have been here all afternoon. We're about to head out." He flashed her a brilliant smile. "I think she needs her dinner."

In response, she stepped even closer, wanting to recapture all the certainty and rightness of the day.

Malcolm's stare easily penetrated her shaky confidence. "Well, have a good evening. I'll see you at the office on Monday, Flynn."

Lauren stared after Malcolm while Flynn gathered up their belongings. Why had she felt so uncomfortable? Obviously, Flynn had seen nothing unusual about Malcolm's sudden appearance.

"What sounds good to you?" Flynn's voice brought her up short. "How about dinner at the Ninety-Fifth, overlooking all of Chicago's beautiful lights?"

"That sounds wonderful," she agreed, and then batted her eyelashes playfully. "But I haven't a thing to wear. You really should take me back to my apartment, Flynn."

"And spoil our special day? No way." His clasp prevented her from walking against the light. "We'll just have something at my place then. I like what you're wearing."

The argument lasted for about three minutes. She wanted to go home. He wanted her to stay. She stayed. Never once did he mention the second break-in or his concern for her safety, but they both realized that was a part of both their decisions.

Flynn couldn't help but wonder how, in the midst of the biggest fiasco of his professional life, he could experience such perfect contentment. But his and Lauren's shared happiness depended on his ability to weather the crisis. So far, nothing had come of his planted lure, and Monday he'd have to try another tack.

"Where are you?" Lauren asked.

They were sitting in the kitchen devouring enormous bowls of store-bought minestrone. Crumbs of flaky French bread covered the table between them. A lighted candle lent atmosphere, and the stereo was playing oldies-but-goodies.

"Just considering my options." He grinned reassuringly and raised his glass of chianti. "Not the Ninety-Fifth, but it'll do."

"You make everything special. Flynn, this was such a wonderful day. . . ."

" 'But' . . . I can hear it in your voice." He leaned over and blew out the candle. "It's not over yet. Take your wine and follow me."

He led her down a darkened hallway and opened a sliding door to a small, screened porch, where a cream colored wicker rocker stood beside a small table with a lamp on it. From the corner, Flynn unrolled a rope hammock which he hooked kitty-corner across the porch. "Sometimes I sleep out here during the summer," he explained. "Grab some pillows."

The hammock shifted precariously, but Flynn showed her how to balance their weight so they could be comfortable together. Then he started the hammock rocking slightly.

His voice deepened and roughened. "I don't want you to go home. I want you to stay with me. . . ."

She shook her head in disagreement.

"At least until we catch the guy in your apartment."

"Well . . ."

His hands caressed her and coaxed her up against him. He began kissing her mouth—light, playful touches. In between each kiss he questioned, not allowing her to answer.

"Stay?"

She could feel her resolve weakening as

her body clamored for more of the delight she had shared with him. "Mmm . . ."

"Stay!"

Finally she pushed him away, setting the hammock into an uneven lurch which caused them to collide together. Breathlessly, she complained, "You won't let me answer."

He shifted them around so they lay side by side.

"You're taking advantage of me," she continued.

"Not until you say you'll stay," he teased. He covered her with an arm and a leg, enveloping her in a rope booby trap. "I don't want you to leave."

Then he kissed her chin, progressing down and under to the softness of her neck. She squirmed in his embrace.

"All right. All right," she capitulated. "But only if we can get out of this contraption."

"Not just yet," he muttered. "I've got you where I want you."

He started the hammock rocking again, as he covered her face and neck with kisses. She kissed him in return, but with no leverage, she was unable to do much more.

Each touch, each kiss enflamed her. Longing for greater fulfillment, knowing it was impossible here on the porch in the hammock, guessing correctly the meaning of his last words, she tried to think of a way to get him out of the hammock. Finally, she grabbed the ropes on either side of them, and with one giant heave dumped him over and onto the floor. Laughing uncontrollably, she landed on top of him.

Flynn, stunned, propped himself up and regarded Lauren with amazement. "I didn't know you were that strong."

"There are a lot of things you still don't know about me," she kidded.

He sprang up and slung her over his shoulder fireman style. "I'm about to find out, though." Then he carried her up the stairs to his bedroom.

The next morning she was able to convince him that she needed to get to her apartment to pack clothes for work and pick up several personal items. Refusing to let her go by herself, he drove her to her building.

Just as she and Flynn were entering the door, Chuck pulled up to the curb and called out to them. Dressed in tennis gear, he sprang out of his Corvette. "There you are, Flynn! I've been trying to beep you all weekend. I took the chance you might be with Lauren."

Flynn's arm dropped from her shoulder. "Don't tell me. More trouble with Blackford."

"Sorry, buddy." Chuck gave them his wide smile, almost apologetically. "A friend of mine in the mayor's office tipped me off that he's calling an emergency meeting first thing Monday morning. Thought I should warn you. Looks like this is it."

Gazing quickly at Flynn, Lauren saw his face grow rigid, the vein throbbing along his jawline.

"Thanks, Chuck. Damn, I'd hoped for more time!"

"You got anything to give him on Monday?" Chuck shifted nervously from sneaker to sneaker. "I don't mind telling you, Flynn. Operation Blackford has me worried."

Something flickered across Flynn's eyes, but it disappeared when he laughed ruefully. "Monday's meeting will be no picnic. But don't worry, I'll think of something." His voice was full of authority, and his words seemed to satisfy Chuck. But not Lauren.

They entered her apartment. It was cool and quiet, almost foreign to her after spending two days with Flynn.

While she packed enough for a few days, unwilling to admit a hope that her stay might be longer, she wondered how she could best help him: Let him talk about it, or help him try to forget it for a while?

"Flynn, what are you going to do?" she asked, her mind made up. Their future wouldn't be clear until some immediate problems were solved. "About the mayor . . . and Councilman Blackford?"

The late afternoon sun was streaming in through her windows, so his face was lost in the glare, but when he moved toward her, she saw that his eyes were forbidding.

"I told you I had a plan. So far it doesn't seem to have netted anyone, but I'll know that for sure tomorrow morning. If it doesn't work, I'll have to think of something else. . . . But I'm not going to let that spoil our day."

He closed the book he had picked up, and Lauren knew he had been studying the pages surrounding the one with Dr. Jamieson's hieroglyphics that had been ripped out by the intruder.

"It doesn't make much sense, does it?" she pointed out quietly. "How could something Dr. Jamieson wrote have any meaning for a common burglar . . . or for some revenge-seeker from Indiana?"

Flynn led her to the couch. "You're right. Maybe we're going at this the wrong way. Let's just review everything we know together, without making any judgments."

Eager to do something, anything, that would resolve the mystery, she grabbed a pen and paper and started listing facts.

"One: My stepfather was indicted and convicted of embezzlement and bribery. Two: I was a witness in that case. Three: When it was finished, I moved up here, and had no problems until . . ."

"Until you met me." Flynn was startled by the thought. Could it be an old enemy of his—someone trying to get to him through

Lauren? "Nothing was going on, no one was harassing you, until you met me."

"It's not your fault," she hastened to reassure him. "Because even before we got . . . close, strange things started to happen."

"Yeah. Your apartment burglary."

"No. Even before that, Flynn. Right after Dr. Jamieson's funeral things started feeling strange. I remember thinking I was being followed—but that was you."

Flynn stood up and paced thoughtfully. "Maybe. Maybe not. My detective says somebody else was following you, too. We're going to try to trap him by having two men watch you: one to protect you, and one to spot the other tail."

"What! Why didn't you tell me this before?" Lauren demanded.

He crossed to her window, gazing at the surveillance post thoughtfully. "All I want is for you to be safe," he said quietly. Safe and with me, he determined silently.

There was such concern in his voice that she rushed to him and put her arms around him. "I know, and I do feel safe. I'm not really upset, just surprised. You have to realize I'm used to looking after myself. Don't keep things from me."

"You're right. I'm sorry." He ran his hands urgently down her back, holding her close, burying his face for a moment in her hair.

He licked at her shell-like ear. "I like this

. . . a lot. But aren't we supposed to be making a list or something?''

Laughing, she pulled out of his arms. "Come sit. Let's finish our list. I'm going to put Dr. Jamieson's memorial service as number four on our list. I met you there. Then, Five: I thought I was being followed."

He looked at her closely. "Lauren, you're almost enjoying this, aren't you?"

She smiled up at him. "It feels better to be trying to do something other than just pretending it will go away."

That's my girl, he thought. He recognized that he loved her. He just hadn't realized how it would grow and deepen day after day.

Sinking down beside her, he stretched his arm along the back of the couch. "The day you got your books and they were in my trunk, my car was almost robbed," he added, recalling the incident for the first time since it had happened.

"I thought of that before." She shook her head. "I've been through all the books that Dr. Jamieson left me. There was nothing unusual but that one page of hieroglyphics."

"All right. What happened next? Your office was vandalized, but nothing was missing—right?"

"Right. It's almost as if someone is seeking something. They've searched my apartment twice, and my office. They've followed me. What will they try next?"

"Don't worry about that. My best man, Taggart, will be with you all the time. And now he'll even have a backup."

"I know you'll protect me." The blaze of trust in her eyes warmed him. Then a frown appeared on her forehead and he wanted to kiss it away.

"But I have this suspicion that I've forgotten something important, Flynn. Or that I should recognize something obvious. But, when I do, we'll understand what is happening."

There was no other way.

The book had been left on the desk the night Dr. Jamieson had died; he'd left it in his will to Lauren; she was an expert on ancient Egypt. It had to be a clue for hero.

Could these few markings have been the evidence the doctor had warned him about? He ran his finger over the hieroglyphics, deliberately smudging them. Unfortunately, he couldn't very well go around asking someone to interpret the marks for him, or just wait until Blackford and the others decided to desert him.

Maybe she hadn't figured them out, but he couldn't take the chance. Sooner or later she would.

It was a shame; she was awfully pretty, and when he first met her ... Well, Flynn, as usual, had gotten everything he wanted. Everything always came easily to him—but not this time. He'd see to that.

And there'd be plenty of other pretty girls to choose from, once he had the power and prestige.

12 Lauren tossed and turned all night. The Egyptian hieroglyphics had come to life, dancing through her dreams. Something was missing, some vital clue she should have understood. Dr. Jamieson had left her that book, that message. He'd assumed she'd be able to decipher it, so she would.

The next morning in the museum parking lot Lauren made another discovery. She didn't want to leave Flynn. She'd never felt like this in her entire life.

"Is something wrong?" Flynn asked, leaning further into the BMW, his hand outstretched to help her.

"No, no," she muttered, closing her fingers tightly around his and stepping out into the parking lot of the Field Museum.

"I'll miss you today," he said, placing his hands lightly on her shoulders.

Surprising herself, she flung her arms tightly around his neck. "I'll miss you, too," she whispered into his throat and felt his arms fold around her. Getting a grip on herself—this just wasn't like her at all—she pulled back.

Flynn cupped her face in his palms, studying her carefully. "There's no need for you to be frightened any longer. Taggart will be right here at the museum with you, and we'll have a backup man when you leave. You're safe."

Drawing a long, quivering breath, she nodded. "I know. I'll be fine. And busy. The pottery seminar is late this afternoon. I'll call you when I'm finished cleaning up."

"I'll be at my office waiting."

Now, to her delight, it was Flynn who didn't want to let go. He clasped her close for one last embrace and a light kiss on the forehead. "We'll do something special tonight."

She watched from the doorway of the employee's entrance until his car was out of sight. Just for a few minutes more she wanted to enjoy the dream-like haze in which she had existed all weekend. Could this much happiness be maintained on a daily basis without mundane things like work intruding?

Then she noticed a plain brown sedan parked opposite the door. A man sat with an open newspaper propped against the steering wheel. For a moment he just stared at her, then he turned back to his paper. Taggart, she surmised. He was in place.

Lauren did a full morning's work on the

collection, assisting with the final placement of all the weapons for the new exhibit.
The display cases had been set up behind a
false wall. Tonight, the case around the
Ship of the Dead in her own collection
would be moved to make way for an elab-
orate display of ornamental daggers, which
would be placed in glass cases lining the
entrance to the exhibit area to draw attention to the new exhibit. There had been a
mix-up in the glass order, so some of the
swords could not be put into their cases until the following day, when the last case
would arrive. For security reasons they
were left stacked in one corner of the storeroom. An enormous Viking shield that
would serve as the doorway, still wrapped
in packing materials, was also waiting to be
mounted in place.

"Lauren, you look radiant!" Bea remarked over lunch, her face beaming. "It's
Flynn, isn't it? He's the one who's brought
the bloom to your cheeks."

Lauren smiled, idly forking through her
julienne salad. "Yes. It is Flynn. We . . . we
straightened out our differences."

Bea nodded in approval. "I knew it!
You're seeing him again."

To Lauren's acute embarrassment, the
image of Flynn in his study, standing gloriously naked before sweeping her up in his
arms, flashed into her thoughts. Hastily
looking down into the ruin of her salad, she
nodded.

"Yes. I . . . I hope to be seeing a lot more of him." Realizing what she had just said, Lauren burst into laughter.

Chuckling along with her, Bea shook her head. "If I didn't know better, dear, I'd think you were intoxicated."

Reaching across the table, Lauren patted Bea's hand. "I am intoxicated, Bea, with happiness." And Lauren realized how true it was. The weekend with Flynn had completely wiped everything else from her mind, so that she didn't even burden Bea with the story of the latest intruder. Somehow, nothing seemed important compared to her time with Flynn.

After lunch, Lauren set to work arranging the cafeteria for the pottery seminar, pulling some of the tables into a *U* shape, facing the instructor's table. She set a newspaper at each place, so that when they worked with the clay the mess could be controlled. The potter from the Art Institute would be bringing the rest of the materials, and he had assured her that the class wouldn't actually be making anything—the clay was just to demonstrate and practice certain techniques.

Even the excitement of the seminar, which she had been anticipating for so many months, couldn't push Flynn to the back of her mind. It seemed forever until they would be together again. Another night with Flynn. How many nights would they have together before they caught whoever

was following her? He had been so sweetly
insistent that she stay with him. Perhaps
she should have put forth more objec-
tions—of course, at the time she had been
half-asleep, her cheek resting against his
warm chest, his hand stroking her back, so
there was really no room for argument. Just
like all this day there had seemed little
room in her thoughts for anything but
Flynn.

Flynn glanced at his watch; the hours
were crawling by. Usually, he was so absorbed in his work that time flew by, but
not today.

Not that he really wanted to stop thinking about Lauren, but he had to focus his
attention on plugging the leak in Operation
Blackford.

The bait hadn't been taken. He would
have heard something by now—the newspaper headlines should have castigated him
royally! There was no way they would have
sat all weekend on the damaging information he'd dropped into the wastebasket.

Which more than likely meant that no
one was going through his trash. So he had
to conclude the maintenance crew was
clean.

That left his secretarial staff. Some of
them had been in the State Attorney's Office for years. Flynn couldn't believe one of
them would do this. Somehow, there was
something he was overlooking, some other

avenue through which information was leaking out. Chuck's security, as good as it had always been, had slipped up this time.

The phone rang, and his secretary announced that John Denis, Blackford's attorney, was on the line. As much as he hated to do it, Flynn had to take advantage of this chance to test Betty.

"Good. This is the call I've been waiting for. Could you bring me in a cup of coffee, please?"

He was only a little disappointed to find out that Councilman Blackford was not interested in testifying for immunity. Of course not! Word had no doubt gotten through to them that the leak was secure.

By the time Betty brought his coffee he had concluded his conversation with Blackford's lawyer and was talking to a dead line.

"So Blackford is prepared to cooperate for immunity," he said, confirming the phony information on the dead telephone line. He watched her reaction carefully out of the corner of his eye.

Either Betty was a great actress, or she wasn't the leak. After he hung up the phone, her only reaction was relief.

"I've been so worried about you, Mr. Fitzgerald."

"Thanks, Betty." He kept up the illusion, the concerned lines across her forehead making him feel like a rat. "But I'd like to keep this development under wraps for a while."

Malcolm pushed open the door. "You've been summoned to the mayor's office. Thought I'd go with you for moral support."

The mayor was alone when Flynn and Malcolm entered his office. Behind his desk, the United States and city of Chicago flags flanked a large oil painting of the office's previous tenant, a reform-minded martyr who had captured the hearts of his constituents. This mayor was eager to do the same.

"Good to see you, Fitzgerald." He led them to a leather grouping by the window overlooking Daley Plaza. Sun glinted off the Picasso sculpture far below.

"This is Malcolm Carlson, also of the D.A.'s office." Flynn explained. "He's been instrumental in developing the case against Councilman Blackford."

"Carlson," the mayor acknowledged briefly. "That's what I've asked you here to discuss. Sit down, gentlemen."

The mayor remained standing by the window for a few moments before crossing the room to lean against his desk. He chose his words with care.

"There's a lot at stake here. I'm concerned how this case reflects on this office." He turned directly to Flynn. "You've been quoted as saying I'm interested in cleaning up the city. Don't put words in my mouth again. I have a press secretary who is very concerned about my image."

He gestured briefly. "Off the record, any hint of impropriety in this city's government involves me. But I have to deal with these people officially. The councilman is flexing his muscles a little, claiming the charges are all political. He's been around City Hall longer than I have, and my people are taking a lot of flak."

Joining them, he sprawled across the small leather couch. The mayor smiled and loosened his tie a little. Flynn couldn't help but be amused; the mayor was just one of the good old boys. Except this good old boy could break him.

"Boys, I know you're having problems, but I have problems, too. The Better Government Association is starting to get in on the act."

"The BGA?" Surprised, Flynn straightened in his chair. "Why's your office involved? They haven't contacted us with an inquiry."

"That's because it's *your* office they're planning to investigate."

Malcolm lunged to his feet, nervously fingering his glasses. "Sir, that can't be allowed right now, not while we're in the middle of this Blackford mess. It'll drain too much man power away from our caseload."

"That's exactly why they're doing it now. This whole Operation Blackford has a real bad stink to it," the mayor went on. "Fitzgerald, you're going to have to bring the grand jury investigation to a successful conclusion quickly or face dismissal."

"But, sir—" Malcolm began.

"Malcolm, the mayor's fully within his rights," Flynn cut in. His eyes met the mayor's in complete understanding. The just-one-of-the-boys pose was gone. This was the man who had fought for and won the right to govern this city. And this was an election year, after all. As Flynn rose to his feet, so did the mayor. "I understand."

"Good. I knew you would."

"Pardon me, sir, but I think you're missing the point here," Malcolm persisted. "Surely you, of all people, know how this city works. It may take some time, but Flynn is the best bet you've got to put an end to the corruption we all acknowledge. Everyone 'in the know' realizes it would be to your best advantage to get rid of Blackford." Malcolm glanced around warily, but Flynn's response was only a lifted eyebrow, although he was taken aback by Malcolm's unusual vehemence. Malcolm might be the pessimist, but he'd never been the aggressor before. Now he was taking on the mayor singlehandedly.

"It's you who doesn't understand, Mr. Carlson. Yes, I know how this city works. That's the problem. And it's working against you now. Your time, gentlemen, is running out."

When they returned from their visit with

the mayor, Flynn set up a strategy session with the FBI for the next day.

Most of the people signed up for the pottery seminar were art teachers at local colleges and high schools. Lauren had eighteen people on her registration sheet; she wasn't expecting a nineteenth.

When Malcolm came through the cafeteria doors she was surprised, but she remembered Flynn's words. Was Malcolm the backup; another person to watch over her?

"Hello, Malcolm," she said pleasantly.

"Lauren." Nodding, he pushed his glasses higher on his nose. "I hope you have room for one more. A friend of mine at the U of C told me about this seminar. I meant to call you about it."

"You've come for the seminar?" Surprise warred with curiosity in her question.

Malcolm's face assumed the look that she had seen once before in his uncle's library—distant and cool. "Why so surprised?"

Lauren smiled apologetically. "I just didn't know you were interested in ancient pottery."

"Lauren, I was very close to Uncle Bernard," he said flatly, as if that answered her question. And, in a way, it did. From his journals, she had learned just how devoted Bernard had been to both Malcolm and Chuck, and they to him. It made sense that

Dr. Jamieson's enthusiasm would have instilled the same interests in the cousins.

Malcolm took a chair near the door, and since there were few places left, Lauren sat beside him.

The instructor was informative and amusing. He had them all pushing and probing their clay as if they were children. To Lauren, squishing the stuff through her fingers, it was almost therapeutic, like kneading dough or scrubbing floors.

When the potter from the Art Institute was talking about how skilled the Etruscans had been in terra cotta and showed an example of an Etruscan earthen vessel decorated with various geometric designs, Lauren became aware of Malcolm's intent concentration. The discussion then turned to an Egyptian earthenware bowl, made between thirty-two hundred and three thousand B.C. It was decorated with an arrangement of animals and hills shaped like pyramids, and Malcolm leaned forward eagerly in his chair.

At the break, he grabbed a Styrofoam cup full of the coffee Lauren had set out, and cornered the potter into a heated discussion.

When the seminar broke up, she had every intention of asking Malcolm if Flynn might have sent him to look after her. But the session ran late, and in the rush of people leaving, Malcolm seemed to disappear. The teachers had so many questions, which

the potter patiently answered, that Lauren
was able to straighten up the room before
the last stragglers left. Then, because the
museum was already closed, she had to
make sure they all got out through the
proper exit.

Thank goodness they were gone, she
thought with relief when the door finally
shut behind the instructor. She was eager
to call Flynn.

She only had to return some equipment
to the storeroom, and then she'd be free to
leave. On the way to the storeroom, she noticed with dismay that there was still a lot
of work to be done on the weapons exhibit.
The glass case had been removed, but the
burial ship still blocked the new entry.
She'd have to get to the museum early the
next morning to supervise its replacement.
It wasn't fragile, but it was one of very
few, and she wouldn't want it damaged in
any way. All the swords were ready for
placement—at least that case had been
completed. She opened the storeroom door
and flipped on the light. The shield was still
in its swathings of bunting on the floor.
She'd have maintenance help her move it in
the morning.

She turned back to the door—and
screamed.

"Malcolm!" Falling back one step, her
hand flew to her throat. "You scared me to
death! I thought you'd left."

"Sorry," he stated flatly. "I was just

wandering around the museum looking at things.''

"In the dark? The museum's closed. Didn't Kevin stop you?"

"I didn't see anyone. There doesn't seem to be anyone here."

Maybe it was because is was so dark and quiet, or maybe it was because Malcolm's flat voice suddenly struck her as alarming, but Lauren retreated further into the storeroom, her ankle brushing against the shield's bunting.

Malcolm followed her.

"Is something wrong, Lauren? You look pale. Can I do anything for you?"

She took a stand beside the shield. "No," Lauren said firmly. "I'm fine. . . . I . . . I guess I'm still surprised at your interest in pottery."

"Why? Everything isn't exactly the way it looks on the surface . . . or anyone, for that matter. People aren't always what they seem. You should know that."

Uneasiness fled in the face of suspicion. Could Malcolm know about her stepfather? About how completely she had been taken in by him?

She looked him squarely in the eyes. "What do you mean by that, Malcolm?"

Shrugging, he pushed his glasses against the bridge of his nose. "Just an observation in general. Uncle Bernard had an uncanny knack for seeing people as they really were. He once told me life was like a chess game.

Some of us are kings, some knights, others pawns." Malcolm's thin lips quirked up at the corners. "In the State Attorney's Office, all I see are snakes. When the powerful fall from grace, it isn't a pretty sight." His interested gaze searched the room. Then he suddenly changed the subject. "I need to go. Could you show me where to leave?"

At the door, he gave her a thin smile. "Flynn's expecting your call. Don't forget."

She leaned against the back of the door, staring into the darkened museum. She had been frightened by Malcolm's sudden appearance, but now those feelings were being replaced by something struggling at the fringes of her memory. It was the same vague uneasiness that had bothered her for days. Life was a chess game? She wondered if Flynn looked at life that way. Should people be used as pawns—needlessly sacrificed for some greater goal? No, he wouldn't feel like that.

Lymond hadn't either. Lauren paused—whatever had made her think of her fictitious hero? Suddenly she remembered the human chess game he had been a part of in *Pawn in Frankincense*, the fourth Dunnett book. The game board on the cartouche! Dr. Jamieson knew of her love for the Lymond books, how she had read and reread them. Was it possible that it all tied in somehow?

The hieroglyphics were a starting point. A starting point! That was it! Those glyphs might only be a clue, not the answer to the puzzle itself. That must be it!

Her cubbyhole office was only down the hallway. The repainting of her regular office upstairs would be finished this week. Now that her mind seemed to be churning with ideas, she attacked the message Dr. Jamieson had left her with a different perspective.

She wrote the symbols in the order they'd been on the page, or as near to it as she could remember. The glyphs were all out of order for Tut's name; perhaps she never should have rearranged them. She studied them again. Maybe if she just read them aloud she'd get a clue.

"Evil. Manifest. Game board. Evil. Lord." It was still confusing. Dr. Jamieson had had such an orderly mind. Why would this be so disorderly?

"Damn!" She pounded her hand on the desk and broke her pencil.

If the book hadn't been right in front of her, she never would have figured it out; as it was, she searched for another pencil, and in doing so, brushed the book to the floor. Automatically, she picked it up. *Game of Kings*.

Malcolm had referred to chess—that was the game of kings. Lauren's fingers trembled. Suddenly everything fell into place. The game board glyph meant chess, and there had been two serpents—two evils. Not just evil manifested, but an evil lord.

She glanced up to her makeshift shelf. All the other Dunnett books were there: *Queens Play, Pawn in Frankincense, The Ringed Castle, Checkmate*. All except, *Disorderly Knights*, the book in which the villain has been unmasked. Is that what the clues were leading to? The unmasking of a villain?

An evil lord, a game player, an evil life: hieroglyphics familiar to any Egyptian scholar, but written out of order to draw her attention, to lead her to another source.

She dialed Flynn's number eagerly.

"Flynn." She was breathless. "I think I've discovered what Dr. Jamieson meant. Those glyphs were just directing me to another source." For good measure, she flipped through each Dunnett book as she spoke.

"Dr. Jamieson was leading me to one of the Dunnett books. I'm sure of it. . . ."

She listened intently to Flynn's instructions, his concern making her smile, but her excitement broke into his words of caution. "I'm all right here. Taggart's outside, and Kevin should have the security system on by now. There's no way anyone could get in here. Come to the employee's entrance where you let me off this morning and I'll have Kevin open up for you. I'll be in the third floor offices."

She was thrilled by her discovery. What kind of message could Dr. Jamieson have left for her?

The faster she found that book, the sooner she'd know. She dialed Kevin's number in the security room, but there was no answer. He must be making his rounds.

She'd go upstairs and phone him from there. She knew the elevators would be shut down, so she crossed the carpeted hallway to the steps, her heels clicking on the marble staircase.

When she reached the great hall, she called out Kevin's name but got only a hollow echo through the darkened space. The floodlights still shone up through Tyrannosaurus Rex; Kevin hadn't been here yet to turn them off. He must be out by the main entrance bringing in the flags. Lauren was so anxious to get up to Bea's office, she didn't bother looking for him.

When she reached the second floor and crossed the carpet to the next stairway she heard sudden noises. Kevin was back. A loud crack proved he had just slammed a door. Good. By the time she found whatever Dr. Jamieson had left for her, he'd be back in the security room and she could call him and tell him to let Flynn in when he arrived.

Disorderly Knights was on Bea's desk, a bookmark halfway through it. Sorry, Bea. I hope you remember your page, Lauren thought as she turned the book upside down and shook it.

Nothing.

Quickly she flipped through the pages and then shook the book again.

Still nothing.

She carefully took off the protective covering, and then the paper jacket itself. There was nothing taped between the layers.

Frustration made her fingers clumsy, and again she let the book fall face-open to the desk. Some of the pages were bent. She lifted it carefully, intending to smooth them out before she closed the covers. That's when she found it . . . by accident.

There was a small space between the hard binding and the pages. Something was there! She couldn't reach it with her fingers, but if she used the eraser end of a pencil very carefully she might be able to budge it. She bent the book back and carefully probed with a pencil from Bea's desk. Her hands were clammy and impatient, but slowly, so very slowly, she felt it move, until finally she dislodged it.

It was a small, folded strip of yellow legal paper. Carefully, she unfolded it until it lay flat on the desk. Dr. Jamieson had listed dates and places including the Art Institute, the Museum of Science and Industry, and the Field Museum. She knew instinctively it was a list of payoffs. And she bet Flynn would see they corresponded with all the leaks in Operation Blackford. She knew it as certainly as she had ever known anything.

This had absolutely nothing to do with her past at all!

And if Dr. Jamieson had this information, that meant only one thing. The leak was one of his nephews.

That would mean real trouble for Flynn.

But trouble was already there in the room with her, settling over her in a formless way like a fog. It didn't have any color, no smell or sound, just a clenching tension of pain and fear as she looked up at the doorway.

"Chuck! What are you doing here?"

He didn't say a word. He simply smiled blindingly, sweetly, straight at her.

13

"What have you got there, Lauren?"

Chuck propped one shoulder against the door frame, filling the whole opening with his presence.

It couldn't be Chuck, Chuck with the choirboy face and smile. . . .

But of course, it had to be Chuck, or why else hide the information in this particular book: *The Disorderly Knights*, where the fair-haired angelic Graham Malett, trusted and beloved knight of Malta, was unmasked as a corrupt, dangerous madman. Dr. Jamieson knew that Chuck would have access to his library and had cleverly hidden the evidence for her to find. He had trusted her to understand his final message. How it must have broken Dr. Jamieson's heart to discover his nephew's complicity. All of this passed through her thoughts in an instant as she sat staring at the eerie smile plastered on Chuck's face. But when the next thought came to her, she blurted it out without realizing the consequences.

"How did Dr. Jamieson uncover your dirty little scheme?"

Chuck straightened and confidently stepped into the office. "So, you figured it out, did you? Very clever." He continued contemptuously, "Uncle Bernard was in on it, of course."

"You're lying!" Lauren shouted, rising to her feet to face him. "Dr. Jamieson was the most honorable man I've ever known. You used him somehow and he discovered it. Is that when he had his last attack? When he confronted you with this evidence? And you just let him die!"

Chuck's bright blue eyes flickered, and an ugly snarl twisted his mouth. "Shut up, you bitch! I didn't want him to die. I could have brought the old man around eventually. But we were on the phone and I couldn't get to him in time."

"Still, he had time to hide the evidence so you couldn't find it." Slowly, Lauren edged from behind the desk, taking the sheet of yellow paper with her, folding it into an even smaller square.

"Yes. But now you've found it for me, Lauren. Give it to me!" he demanded, threading his way around the chairs.

Shaking her head, she backed toward the windows, her eyes darting around the office. He stood between her and the only doorway.

"Give it to me!" he demanded again, stepping closer.

"No!" She thrust her hands behind her back, protecting the precious square of paper. She wouldn't let him get it, at any cost. As she backed away from him, the residual warmth of Bea's glass teapot singed her knuckles.

Bea always turned off the hot plate when she left, but the water, after simmering all day, still retained some heat now.

Shifting the note to her left hand, she gripped her right hand around the handle of the teapot. Her heart pounded in her throat, but she waited for the right moment.

"Damn it! Give me the paper before I have to hurt you!" Chuck snarled, grabbing for her.

At that exact moment, she flung the water in his face, sending the pot crashing to the floor.

Blinded for an instant, Chuck stumbled back, and she shoved past him, making it to the door and out into the museum.

"Kevin!" she screamed.

The only light was behind her in Bea's office. Lauren knew the museum's floor plan as well as she knew her own small apartment, so she fled into the darkness. Her heels echoed on the marble steps as she stumbled down them in haste and fear. She had to get to the main floor. All she had to do was reach Kevin in the security room.

"Kevin!" she called again.

She could hear Chuck pounding down

the steps behind her. He was at least one flight behind. Why didn't Kevin answer? Surely he could hear her.

Around the next curve of stairs, light shone from Stanley Field Hall. The floodlights shining up through the skeleton of Tyrannosaurus Rex were still on. That wasn't right; Kevin always turned the spotlights off at night.

As soon as she reached the foot of the stairs, she understood. Past a certain point, degrees of terror are meaningless. Lauren had reached that stage now. Kevin lay in a huddled heap next to the velvet rope protecting the bones of Tyrannosaurus Rex.

"Oh, Kevin," she sobbed.

He must have leaned over to switch off the floodlights. He'd succeeded in turning one out, but before he could reach the others, Chuck had shot him. That was the bang Lauren had heard.

She ran forward to his motionless body. His blood was wet and sticky on her hands. She touched his still warm cheek, and gave a sob of joy when she felt the faint flutter of his pulse beneath her fingers. "You're still alive, thank God," she whispered, and then stopped, trying not even to breathe when she heard Chuck descend the stairs to her level.

She had to get help. For Kevin. For herself. She stuffed the folded yellow paper deeply into her pocket and kicked off her shoes.

Padding noiselessly back before Chuck's steady advance, she crouched behind a black display case, her palms pressed against the cold marble floor.

Chuck stopped by Kevin's body and glanced down at her shoes. He seemed relaxed and he was smiling, as if he had all the time in the world. Time to find her and get the piece of paper. He wouldn't let anything stand in his way now. She had fully understood that the instant she saw Kevin's body.

Chuck's face suddenly set in an odd half smile as he reached inside his blue blazer and pulled out a small black gun.

Dizzy with tension and fear, Lauren squeezed her eyes shut for a moment, forcing her mind to clear. She needed desperately to plan. Her life depended on it.

When she opened her eyes again, Chuck was gone. Frantically, she looked around from her crouched position. Where was he? Behind her? She twisted around; nothing but shadowy, unmoving shapes.

That was when she remembered the opening—one of the newest additions to the museum. The entrance from the main hall to the mummy's tomb in the basement. Chuck might not even realize it was there. All she had to do was make it down through the chamber and out into the collection. The employee's entrance was nearby, and Taggart was in that parking lot. In the time it would take Chuck to go around by the regular stairs, she could be free.

Or she could stay right where she was, hope Chuck didn't find her, and pray that Flynn would get here soon.

Utter silence surrounded her as she debated. When Kevin moaned, the sound tore into her. He couldn't wait. She had to get help now.

Her heart was in her throat, nearly suffocating her, but she jumped up and raced toward the opening. With a surge of adrenaline, she nearly fell through the beginning of the corridor entrance into the tomb as a bullet whizzed by her forehead. Several more wild shots followed, embedding themselves in the marble pillar just beyond the opening.

Sick with fear, she forced her hands to be steady, sliding closed the hidden door and snapping the latch.

The sarcophagus chamber was usually the last room of the tomb complex, preceded by other rooms containing shrines and funeral equipment, and by a long corridor which led to the outer exit in the face of the cliff. The Field Museum had replicated this well; in fact, Lauren had helped design it. The doorway, made to look as authentic as possible, had sloping sides and a squared lintel. It opened onto a long, winding corridor which led downward to the basement and the reproduced tomb in the Egyptian Collection.

She knew right where she was. When the room was lighted, the stone walls blazed with carnelian, lapis, and gold. There were verses to the gods in hieroglyphics, and a painted scene which showed Osiris, Lord of the Westerners, seated on a throne, judging the dead, his ebony face haloed by his oddly shaped crown. She could use some godly help now, she thought wildly.

She stood for an instant, swaying in the dark stone corridor. Then she heard Chuck scratching at the door. The lock has been left over from the construction, when the museum had to be certain no one would fall into the hole. Another shot sounded, muffled through the heavy door. The door rattled violently, but the lock held.

She started down the steadily sloping floor. When the steps began, she grasped the railing which was fitted into the walls, her fingers squeezing around the wood.

Progress down the long corridor in absolute blackness was nearly nightmarish. She knew Chuck would not be able to break through the door behind her. But where was he? Did he know where this led? Would he be waiting for her in the mummy's tomb?

Nothing waited for her at the end of the corridor but more darkness. She felt along the walls, smooth under her palms at first but growing slightly rougher. She was at the paintings now, the conventional scenes of mortuary gods weaving a web of ritual protection around the sleeper in the tomb.

She walked forward, her arms out-stretched, and touched the giant stone box which stood as high as her head; the carved and inscribed sarcophagus. It filled the center of the tomb. At its base was a wooden box containing cloth whose gold and silver threads shimmered, even in the darkness.

She groped to her right. Yes, here was the gilded chest carved with flowers, which meant she was near the basement entrance to the tomb. Her bare foot touched something and it rustled; the reed basket of papyrus scrolls.

All she had to do now was walk through the entrance.

Footsteps echoed into the chamber. Paralyzed for a moment with an icy shock of fear, Lauren realized Chuck was waiting for her at the collection.

He was here in the basement with her.

If she stepped through the entrance she would be a perfect target, for the sensory-activated lights would go on, illuminating the tomb. Did he know that, too?

Except she knew where not to step, how to avoid the sensors. Hugging the right wall, she took three tiny steps, then holding her breath, she took one giant step forward. She was out, and the automatic light hadn't come on. If Chuck was far enough away, she might still make it to the door by the parking lot.

In her excitement, her elbow brushed against the glass case of Egyptian jewelry which sat right outside the mummy's tomb, making an almost imperceptible noise.

"Lauren!" Chuck's eerie whisper echoed through the silent, still room.

Her heart was pounding like a drum. How could Chuck not hear it? If he would just speak again, she could tell where he was, and somehow she would lure him further and further into the collection and away from the door. Then she could slip out and reach Taggart.

"Lauren, where are you? Come on now. I'm not going to hurt you," he whispered again, so near to her that she let out an involuntary yelp and backed up in a running two-step.

He cursed and passed by her so closely she could smell his after-shave. Luckily, he was no better at locating sounds in the dark than she was.

Then Lauren heard Chuck's low, soft laugh, and she froze in fear. He was coming back. He was moving slowly down the corridor between the glass cases, but now he had his arms stretched wide, feeling for her. She could hear his palms smacking against the cases. There was nowhere for her to go.

She shrunk back, surprised there was no glass case behind her. Of course, the case had been moved, but the low wooden burial barge, the ship of the dead, was still in place. The mummified wood of the barge bit into her hands.

Afraid to breathe, she slid noiselessly over the low side and pushed her body tightly into the bottom of the barge. She could feel her heartbeat vibrating in every inch of her body.

When Chuck went by her, she would wait for the right moment—when he was searching for her between the pottery cases in the back of the collection—and then go for the door.

How much time had passed since her call to Flynn? He would be here soon. Please, Flynn, hurry, she prayed.

Flynn's car shrieked to a halt next to Taggart's in the museum parking lot.

"Taggart! What's going on?" he called across the short space separating them.

It wasn't until he knocked at the window that Flynn realized why Taggart wasn't answering.

He wasn't just leaning his head back against the headrest; he was out cold. Flynn could feel the knot on his skull, but Taggart's pulse was strong and steady. He'd be all right.

"Fitzgerald."

Flynn twirled around, adrenalin pumping, ready to spring, but it was only Taggart's backup, the man Taggart always referred to as Larry. "There's trouble, Fitzgerald."

Flynn nodded, pushing his fingers through his hair. "Taggart will be all right."

"Yeah, I know. I already checked on him. I couldn't do anything, though, because the girl hasn't come out yet. I didn't want her to be unprotected."

"She's still in there alone?"

"Yeah. The place is shut up tighter than a drum. I couldn't get in."

Flynn was already running across the parking lot before he remembered to yell back, "Call for help!"

Lauren was inside. But where was Kevin? Why hadn't he heard Larry trying to get in?

He pounded frantically on the heavy door. The fact that Kevin didn't answer chilled Flynn to the marrow.

He wasted no time jimmying the lock. When the door finally gave, Flynn pushed it wide. If this action set off alarms in every police station in Chicago that was just fine with him.

Swiftly, he moved past the Egyptian Collection toward the stairs. He couldn't make out anything in the darkness, so he stopped for a moment to allow his eyes to adjust.

Then he heard a furtive rustle, and a heartbeat later the mummy's tomb suddenly illuminated, clearly identifying the man standing in its entrance.

"Chuck!"

His best friend turned toward Flynn

with bright blue eyes shining out of his tanned face.

"Chuck, what are you doing here?"

Chuck beamed at him cordially. Standing there, tall and relaxed, his golden hair slightly mussed, Chuck looked so normal that the preposterous notion that had blazed into Flynn's mind died.

"Thought I'd check up on Lauren's protection. She's . . . she's . . . up on the third floor."

"Yeah, I know. Something's going on. You sure you're okay? The security man is missing and Taggart was out cold in the parking lot." Flynn stepped forward. "Check around, will you? I'm going up to Lauren."

A muffled sob drew both men's attention. Lauren's fingers curled over the top of the funeral ship. She was having trouble pulling herself out of the deep smooth-sided boat.

"Lauren, what . . ."

"Flynn, look out, he has a gun!" Lauren gasped.

Flynn's eyes darted back to where Chuck still smiled as he pointed a small black gun straight at Flynn's abdomen.

"Chuck, what the hell is this?"

"You mean the gun?" Chuck asked calmly, straightening his arm and raising it to point it at Flynn's heart.

Lauren screamed at the same instant Chuck pulled the trigger. There was a click.

Involuntarily, Flynn recoiled. Then slowly he straightened, his muscles rigid with shock as he stared into Chuck's face.

His friend's laugh echoed through the shadows. "So I make a few mistakes," he said belligerently. "No more bullets in the damn thing." With a violent swipe of his arm, he threw the useless gun aside and it went clanging across the marble floor.

"Talk to me, Chuck. We can work this out. Whatever it is." Flynn tried to modulate his voice, at the same time sending silent signals to Lauren to stay where she was.

But she didn't pay any attention to him. She finally succeeded in getting some leverage and flung herself out of the boat.

Chuck glanced at her and backed quickly toward her, stepping away from the tomb entrance, throwing the room into darkness again.

Flynn sprang after him, but was too late. He could barely make out the two shadows. It seemed Lauren was pressed against the wall, and Chuck stood between her and a doorway.

"Stay back, Flynn! Or I'll have to hurt her!" Chuck shouted.

Stopping halfway across the room, Flynn called out, "Lauren, Chuck, what's going on?"

"He's the leak, Flynn! Dr. Jamieson left evidence in one of my books."

"Shut up!" Chuck shoved her to the floor.

"Chuck, what the hell are you doing!" Stunned, Flynn ran forward.

"I said, stay back!" Chuck's warning stopped Flynn again. Chuck meant it. If Flynn moved any closer, he might hurt Lauren.

Flynn took a deep breath before speaking quietly. "You're the leak? Why?" He had to get him talking.

"She figured it all out," Chuck said almost pleasantly. "An enterprising young woman, Uncle Bernard's Lauren, don't you think?"

Flynn shook his head, still not quite able to believe what was happening. "Chuck, I don't understand."

"That's just the point, Flynn." Chuck's voice was taut with anger. "You should understand. But I'm just so much smarter than you. That's why I'm tired of being in your shadow."

It was then that Flynn finally grasped the enormity of Chuck's plan. "You deliberately sabotaged Operation Blackford to ruin my career."

"I was launching *my* career." Now Chuck's voice mocked in earnest. "There are powerful people willing to help me, Flynn. There's no limit to how far my career can go now."

"Except I know. And so does Lauren.

What are you going to do, silence us both?" Flynn asked coldly.

"Dr. Jamieson knew. That's what killed him. I have the proof," Lauren said quietly.

"Shut up! I told you I didn't mean for him to die!" Chuck snarled, moving in front of Lauren so Flynn could no longer see her.

"Christ, Chuck! Not Bernard!"

"No!" Chuck's voice changed almost to a sob. "I loved the old man. You know that, Flynn! He died of a heart attack. I never thought he'd figure out I was using him to deliver information. I told him it was an undercover assignment for the office."

In the moment that Chuck's attention centered on Flynn, Lauren crept inside the doorway and reached for one of the swords stacked on the work table. But Chuck turned and caught her, forcing her to release the sword to him.

By the time Flynn reached them, his eyes had adjusted to the darkness. He saw Chuck shift the sword in his hands, his face twisted into a snarl.

"But now I have to finish it." Chuck picked another sword and tossed it toward Flynn. It clattered to the floor at Flynn's feet. "Pick it up!"

Lauren stood stock-still against the wall. Chuck advanced toward Flynn, posturing with the blade. Flynn's hands balled in fists at his side.

"Chuck, put the sword down. I'm not going to fight you. . . . Good God, man, come to your senses!"

An odd half smile froze on Chuck's face. Lauren inched along the wall and reached up, flipping on the storeroom lights.

For the first time, Flynn saw Chuck's face clearly, and what he saw convinced him that Chuck was crazed. The choirboy smile had turned to a snarl; the brilliant blue eyes were dilated in frenzy.

"You won't fight me, Flynn? We'll see about that."

Even as Flynn leaped to stop him, Chuck grabbed Lauren's outstretched arm and lifted the sword, slashing wildly.

14

Lauren gripped the wound as she slid to the floor. Blood seeped through her fingers, and it hurt like hell. Grabbing the hem of her skirt, she pressed it tightly to her arm, trying to stop the crimson flow.

Through a filmy haze she heard Flynn's growl, saw him stoop to pick up the sword at his feet and recklessly charge at Chuck. An Alexandrian sword, she thought abstractly, a sword used to carve out a great empire. And Chuck's was Turkish—twelfth century.

Chuck easily parried Flynn's rushed offense. "*Tsk, tsk*. Emotions have no place in dueling, E. Flynn."

Lauren realized she was slipping in and out of consciousness from the pain and loss of blood. She had to control herself enough to reassure Flynn, so that he could regain his own control. She leaned her head back to take in slow, steady breaths of air. She was in the storeroom, leaning against the Viking shield. If she could just pull off some of the cotton batting that protected it, she could tie off the cut on her arm and try to go for help.

Flynn was calling her name, rather desperately she thought. She had to answer him, let him know she was all right. She pressed her fingers tightly over the gash and tried to steady herself.

"I'm okay." The words came out in a croak, loud enough to distract Chuck momentarily. Flynn was able to pivot him around and get closer to her.

"Lauren, get out of here!"

She knew she wouldn't be able to move. She'd already lost enough blood so that it pooled beneath her arm.

"I'm not sure I can," she gasped, trying desperately to keep the panic out of her voice.

Flynn warily eyed his opponent, whose blade taunted.

"No one's going anywhere, Flynn," Chuck almost cackled. "If you want to save her, you'll have to defeat me first."

The light from the storeroom cast grotesque shadows into the Egyptian Collection. Lauren found it easier to follow the huge shadows of the men reflected on the wall than to try to focus on the men themselves. Flynn seemed to hesitate for a moment before walking out into a clear aisle. He brought his sword up to a formal salute—just as he'd done the other time she'd watched them fence. He had barely beaten Chuck then. Could he do it now?

Her fingers froze in the act of pulling at the batting as the swords clanged together for the first time, echoing loudly. If Flynn should lose, there would be nothing, no one to stop Chuck but herself.

The swords beat together, causing tiny sparks to flash in the darkened room. Occasionally, Lauren would hear one of the men bump into a exhibit case. Or a sword would slice against nothing, slashing through the air with a tremendous *whoosh*.

The duelers were out of sight, not even their shadows remaining to show her the battle. But she could hear the desperate footsteps and the occasional loud clanking of their blades.

Then their was a deadly chuckle. Lauren ripped at the batting and forced a pad over her cut. Grabbing awkwardly at the long cotton fibers with her free hand, she managed to tie them securely in place. Slowly, she gripped the shield, pulling herself to her feet.

Where were they? The museum had grown unbelievably quiet. Lauren could only assume that Flynn and Chuck were playing a deadly game of cat and mouse. What could she do to help?

Her legs wouldn't support her any longer. She crumpled down to the floor, dislodging the shield, and it fell with a tremendous clang, partially blocking the doorway.

When her ears stopped ringing she heard the duel again.

Steel rang against steel. They were coming closer. She could see them now.

"Thought you could escape." Chuck's voice sounded almost mechanical. "I've already been through this basement once in the dark. You don't stand a chance, E. Flynn. Remember, I'm the one with the photographic memory."

"But I'm a better swordsman," Flynn shot back. "Remember that, Chuck, and give up now. I don't want to hurt you. I want to help."

"Help! Sure, like you helped me in law school. You were *Review* editor, I only got to be on staff." He carefully maneuvered his sword closer toward Flynn's body. "Help me! You mean help yourself. Remember Mary Jane? I saw her first, but she only wanted to date you. Like how you got the title in the D.A.'s office and I got all the work. Hell, even Malcolm got more recognition than me. The old man always said Malcolm was the one with the real brains in the family."

Flynn stepped over an object on the floor. Lauren focused on it—it was the empty gun. Useless. It had shot Kevin and tried to kill her, but now it was empty. Or so Chuck claimed. Maybe he'd made another mistake.

Back and forth the shadows lunged. Each man was tiring. Chuck had stopped taunting. Flynn couldn't even try to calm him any longer.

Lauren wanted to get to the gun. She rolled onto her knees and, cradling her injured arm, started to halfcrawl under the shield to get it.

"Get back where you're safe!" Flynn yelled.

How could he fight and watch her at the same time? She'd have to give up on the gun to protect him—so he could concentrate on Chuck.

"The bleeding's stopped, Flynn. I'll be all right now," she called out. Chuck's cry of rage stopped her words. The madman out there wasn't Chuck anymore. Lauren hoped Flynn realized that, too.

They had circled warily, wearily, for several minutes. Lauren could see the reflected light from the blades piercing the gloomy basement. They'd been at it longer now than the practice duel she'd witnessed. These were heavy battle swords, not the light French épées. How long would Flynn's strength hold out?

The swords came up to cross again. This time she could see they were both holding their hilts with two hands. Chuck swung wildly, the force of the miss pulling him off balance. Oddly, Flynn did not press his advantage.

He's an enemy, Flynn, she thought frantically. Forget he was your friend. It's our only hope.

The finesse of battle had been abandoned for strength. Brute strength. Bashing the swords together, trying to keep their footing, Lauren could hear each of them panting.

Flynn cursed and dropped his guard. Chuck charged in, swiping the sword diagonally down as Lauren gasped. Only Flynn's somersault roll saved his life.

Chuck laughed again—the high, keening cry of a man on the brink of insanity. "It's my turn now, Flynn!"

Flynn's sword flickered in front of him. He drove steadily forward, pushing Chuck away from the storeroom and from Lauren. Back, back into the recreated tomb.

The light from the tomb flashed into the collection. Lauren's eyes adjusted automatically, but she knew Flynn would be momentarily blinded.

Chuck must have seen it in the blank face confronting him. He could taste victory. With a triumphant cry, he danced toward Flynn, stepping lightly, holding his sword steady. There was no sound to give Flynn a clue as to where he'd attack next.

Lauren's breath caught. What could she do to help him?

"Flynn!" she screamed a warning. He feinted left and instinctively dove to the right, behind the ship of the dead.

Chuck's crow of triumph turned to a wail of despair.

"Chuck," Flynn pleaded. "Give it up. We're friends. We can work it out."

"Never!" Chuck's blade swung in a circle, almost as if he'd lost control of himself. "This is a fight to the finish. To the finish! Understand that, Flynn. And when I've gotten rid of you, I'll finish off dear Lauren. Once I have that paper, I'm home free."

Again, the shadows showed the two men crossing swords. Lauren pulled the paper out of her pocket. The evidence had been hidden before, she would hide it once more. She struggled to her feet and stumbled to the work table. Chuck would never be able to find the evidence Dr. Jamieson had gone to so much trouble to get to her. She'd see to that.

There was an English sword-stick with a secret compartment in the pile of weapons.

If Flynn didn't win, perhaps she could use the whereabouts of the evidence to bargain with until help arrived. Where was Taggart? And the backup? Oh, Flynn, her mind cried, my love—it all depends on you.

She picked up a small marking pen and scrawled across the paper, "Chuck Jamieson." Then she pushed it into the sword-stick and clicked the compartment shut.

Unable to stand any longer, she crawled back to her watch post by the door.

The fight was progressing in earnest

now. Tension enveloped her. She couldn't remain in the storeroom, safe, isolated from Flynn any longer. She had to try to help him.

Grabbing one of the smaller swords, she crawled under the shield and out into the collection.

Flynn was concentrating so hard on Chuck that he missed her movements. But Chuck saw her crawling silently, steadily, out toward them.

"Get back, dear Lauren. I'll attend to you later," he raged. "Unless you want to see the almighty Flynn defeated."

Lauren was close enough to hear Chuck gasp for breath, smell his fear, feel his hatred. But she couldn't move at all; no closer to him to stop the fight, and no farther away, to safety.

Chuck took a menacing step toward her.

"No!" Flynn cried. He snapped his blade clumsily, trying to draw Chuck's attention back to himself. "The fight's over here with me, Chuck."

Flynn could see that Lauren's surge of activity had completely drained her. Blood had soaked through her makeshift bandage; her face was white with pain. But her lips were pressed together with indomitable determination. He knew she wouldn't be able to get away safely. He was the only one who could protect her now, the only hope for them both.

He advanced toward Chuck, pushing him

away from Lauren and back into the darkness beyond the mummy cases. The sword was heavy in his hands, his breath coming in short bursts, but he knew his own skill and realized Chuck must be tiring, too. Instinctively, he rose to the balls of his feet, calling forth every last bit of strength as he began to feint—delicately flicking his sword from side to side.

With his bold play, he seemed to lose all sense of caution. He juggled the sword carelessly between his hands, giving Chuck multiple opportunities to lunge and finish the duel.

Chuck eyed him, confused. "What trick are you up to now?"

Flynn continued advancing. His sword seemed to jump from hand to hand. His left foot steadied, then with no warning, his right arm extended full length and his sword ran up the blade of Chuck's sword until the hilts were locked. They stood inches away from each other—toe to toe, wrist to wrist.

Their eyes locked in combat as mortal as any with sword. Flynn leaned hard into his blade, exerting the full pressure of his body against Chuck's strength.

Then suddenly Flynn went limp. Chuck was overbalanced as he tilted forward, and Flynn, disengaged, threw Chuck's sword into the display case of Etruscan pottery, shattering the glass.

"Damn you!" Chuck screamed, then began to sob incoherently, crumbling to his knees.

Taking deep, painful breaths, Flynn held him carefully at bay under the point of his sword. Chuck didn't even look at him. He simply curled up into a ball, burying his face in his hands, and sobbed. Flynn felt like he was going to be sick. Stepping back two paces, he turned to Lauren.

Suddenly, lights flooded the basement.

Policemen filled the aisles, blocking Flynn's access to Lauren, but, dropping the weapon, he pushed them aside to kneel beside her.

"Lauren, love . . ."

She gave him a weak smile and then looked beyond him, her eyes widening. Flynn turned just in time to see Chuck being handcuffed. He was still sobbing like a child when two policemen led him away.

When he turned back, Lauren's eyes were closed. "Lauren!" Frantically looking around, he yelled, "Where are the damn paramedics!"

Taggart appeared at his side. "Easy, Flynn. They're upstairs with the guy who was shot. Someone will take a look at her in a minute." He shook his head sheepishly, fingering the lump on his forehead. "Oldest trick in the book and I fell for it. Good thing you and Larry were there to back me up."

"Don't worry, Taggart. How could any of us have guessed it was Chuck all along?"

He could still hardly believe it. Memories of Chuck as he had always known him crowded into his mind, but he pushed them away. Right now, Lauren's welfare was paramount. He ran his hands urgently over her body. She seemed to be all right except for the gash in her arm, which was bleeding steadily again.

"I'm not waiting for the paramedics. I'll take her to the ambulance." Gently, he slid his hands under her body and lifted her up into his arms, holding her close. Her head fell against his shoulder and he pressed a reassuring kiss on her forehead. "Taggart, tell the police I'll be back to give my statement as soon as I make sure Lauren's on the way to the hospital."

She didn't move as he carried her upstairs and out the employees' entrance to where an ambulance waited. As he laid her gently on the stretcher, she opened her eyes. "Flynn . . ."

He raised her hand to his lips and kissed it softly. "You're going to be all right, Lauren. I'll join you at the hospital as soon as I can."

She turned her head quickly from side to side. "Kevin?"

Stroking her cheek, he calmed her. "He's all right. He'll be in the ambulance with you."

She smiled then, and he kissed her again. "You're something, you know that, Miss Michaels."

They came to take her away, but her cry stopped them. "Flynn, wait!" She squeezed his hand, her eyes wide. "The evidence. I hid it in the English sword-stick in the storeroom. It has a secret compartment."

A rush of love so strong it weakened him made him steal one last kiss. "I'll be there soon, love."

He stood watching the ambulance pull away, sirens wailing. Then he turned back to the museum. Taggart waited for him in the doorway.

"I just heard they took Chuck to the hospital psych ward." Taggart shook his head. "I've seen it all, Flynn. But this is tough . . . especially for you."

"Yeah." Flynn threaded his fingers through his hair, taking a deep breath. He knew what he had to do. "Let's get this over with, Taggart. I know where the evidence is hidden. Before I turn it over to the police and give them my statement, I have to make a phone call."

Taggart's cool eyes held understanding. "Malcolm?"

"Yeah, I've got to tell him. I just don't understand any of this, Taggart. How could we all have been so blind? He must have carried around an enormous amount of resentment for a long time."

They started back inside to the store-room. Policemen swarmed everywhere. Taggart silently motioned them back, away from Flynn, giving him a moment to collect his thoughts.

The evidence was right where Lauren had told him it would be. In spite of her injury and the obvious pain she was in, she'd thought to hide the evidence. She'd risked her life to help him.

Lauren had written Chuck's name on the crumpled yellow sheet, but Bernard Jamieson's precise hand had recorded places and dates that covered a period of several months. Flynn immediately recognized a couple of them, confirming his suspicions about a long-standing conspiracy. When he turned the paper over and saw blood, Lauren's blood, he found his hand trembling.

Taggart leaned over his shoulder to study the paper. "This what you needed?"

"Yes. I can't believe this has been going on for so long. No wonder Chuck was desperate." He folded the paper into a deliberate square. "He would have killed Lauren for this—there's no doubt."

"He's a sick man, Flynn. You've got to remember that." Taggart beckoned a police captain over. "He's not the same person as your old school friend."

Flynn turned the evidence over to the

captain, who'd already tagged the gun and the swords. After giving his statement, he left Taggart to attend to the details. The most important thing now was to make sure Lauren was all right.

15 Lauren had always hated hospitals, and her fear of them had worsened since her mother's death. Only Flynn could have convinced her to get into the ambulance, even though she'd been bleeding profusely.

Watching the emergency-room doctors work desperately on Kevin until he went to the O.R. had been a nightmare. The staff wouldn't tell her anything. They just put her in a little curtained area, where an attendant helped her to change into a hospital gown.

Shortly afterward, a doctor arrived and with very little deliberation gave her two shots of painkillers. Then he cleaned the wound and sutured it. She questioned him, too, but he had no information on Kevin. Lying there, the worry and tension and fear finally overcame her; tears began rolling down her cheeks. When the curtain rustled, she angrily brushed them away.

"Bea!" Lauren sat up and was immediately enveloped in Bea's soft embrace. Now the tears flowed freely.

Bea patted her gently. "Lauren, dear, it's all right. Let it all out."

Hiccoughing softly, Lauren pulled away, rubbing her eyes. "How did you know I was here?"

Holding tightly to Lauren's uninjured hand, Bea urged her back down onto the pillow and pulled up a stool. "It's *our* collection you were playing Wonder Woman in, remember? The police contacted the museum administrator, who of course called me, and I came right over."

"I'm so glad you're here, Bea. It was just awful."

"Tell me, dear. It helps to talk about it."

Bea was right. It helped to put all the anger and confusion and fear into words, but when Lauren was finished, Bea looked pale.

"You could have been killed."

Shaking her head, Lauren managed a tiny smile. "Flynn wouldn't have let anything happen to me."

That admission brought color back to Bea's cheeks. "That's right, and don't you forget it. Between me and your Flynn, we'll see that everything is going to be just fine."

The hospital finally transferred her to a private room, and Bea stayed until Lauren was hooked up to an I.V. and settled comfortably.

"I'll be back first thing in the morning,"

she declared. "You get some rest now. I guarantee everything will seem better in the morning. Can I bring you anything?"

After Bea had finally left, Lauren reached behind her head to buzz for a nurse. It wasn't easy to function with one arm wrapped up like a mummy, and an I.V. in the other.

In a very short time a nurse poked her head in the door. "What do you need, Miss Michaels?"

"The man who was admitted with me, Kevin Lawrence, is he still in surgery? Could you find out for me?"

"Just a minute. I'll check."

The door swung shut and the P.A. announced that visiting hours were over. Groggily, she realized that Flynn wouldn't be able to come to see her tonight. But it was probably for the best. Her head would be clearer tomorrow morning. The doctor had told her they were putting something in the I.V. to relax her and help diminish the pain from the stitches in her arm.

She could tell the sedative was already working. She felt totally limp, and her mind was beginning to get fuzzy around the edges. The whole episode was starting to seem unreal. All the fear, anger, and confusion was dissipating before whatever cure-all was dripping into her veins.

The only thing that really mattered was that Flynn had arrived in time and they were both alive. He had been so tender, so caring. And he had called her love. She couldn't seem to stop thinking of that. And that he had saved them all. Now, if only . . .

The door swung open and the same nurse peeked in.

"Mr. Lawrence is out of surgery and listed in satisfactory condition. Get some rest now, Miss Michaels."

The last dread vanished from her mind. Kevin would be all right. Chuck wasn't a murderer, whatever else he was.

There was nothing hazy or fuzzy about her feelings for Chuck. She would never forget how he had looked in defeat. She wasn't a psychiatrist, but anyone could see that he was sick, and not only with greed and jealousy. He'd curled himself up into a little ball, babbling on and on about being too clever to be caught. It was pathetic to realize a mind could destroy itself to that extent. However, she couldn't find it in her heart just yet to feel sorry for him.

It was more than just because of what he had done to her, or even to Flynn. He had betrayed Dr. Jamieson, the man who had loved him as a father. And used him in a way very much like her stepfather had used her. Dr. Jamieson's friendship had helped heal her, and she hoped that in some small way she had repaid him by uncovering the truth.

She still couldn't quite believe she'd unraveled the hieroglyphic message. It had been one last scholarly task brilliantly conceived by Dr. Jamieson—and she hadn't failed him. She felt good about that.

Good and sleepy. She yawned, but was unable to stretch very far with all the paraphernalia hanging from her. Maybe she'd just close her eyes. The sooner she slept the night away, the sooner Flynn would be here.

Flynn hoped that by some miracle the press hadn't gotten hold of this story yet. But when the squad car, graciously made available by the on-site captain, dropped him at the hospital, flashbulbs popped in his face. All the television networks were waiting for him.

How could their sources work so quickly? He was accustomed to microphones and cameras, but tonight it was nearly impossible to keep cool. The din was overwhelming. For the first time in his career, Flynn out-shouted the reporters surrounding him.

"One question at a time, or no interview!"

In the moment of shocked silence that followed, Flynn pointed. "Bill, what's your question?"

"What exactly happened at the Field Museum tonight?"

Flynn cursed silently. So many people to protect—yet the public had a right to know. "The perpetrator of a conspiracy to undermine the grand jury investigation of Councilman Blackford was discovered and apprehended. The District Attorney's office will ask for an indictment in that case tomorrow."

"And the perpetrator's name?" Bill continued.

"Chuck Jamieson, a member of my own staff. This conspiracy was uncovered due to the dedication of some civic-minded civilians."

From beyond the lights, a woman's voice called, "These civilians, are they the two individuals who were admitted to this hospital earlier this evening? Can you give us their names and the extent of their injuries?"

"That's why I'm here, to check up on their progress. A hospital spokesman will be out to advise you as soon as possible, and my office will issue an official statement tomorrow at eight A.M."

Flynn turned to go, but over the hubbub one newsman shouted, "Is Lauren Michaels one of those civilians? And is it true you are personally involved with her?"

That was the final straw. Flynn swung around and glared in the direction of the question. "Miss Michaels' only involvement in this case is accidental, although, as it turns out, she is its true heroine. Our personal relationship is none of your damn business!"

Pushing past them, he flung open the glass doors and stepped inside the hospital.

He shouldn't have lost control like that. Now Lauren's name would be speculated upon endlessly in the papers.

A brawny security guard blocked his way. "No reporters allowed, sir. And visiting hours are over."

Flynn tensed. After all he'd been through this night, he wasn't going to let anyone stop him from seeing Lauren. He began, "I'm not . . ." when Malcolm stepped out of the elevator.

"This is family," Malcolm assured the guard and led Flynn into the waiting area.

Flynn grasped his shoulder. "Have you seen him?"

Nodding, Malcolm stepped away, sinking into a chair. "They have him up in the psych ward. He's had a complete breakdown." The hand Malcolm used to push his glasses higher on his nose shook. "What happened to him, Flynn? It doesn't seem fair. He had everything going for him. . . ."

"I'm not sure we'll ever understand it completely." Flynn sat beside him, wanting to somehow ease the shock and pain, but not sure of the right words. "Now he'll get the help he needs."

Perhaps that was the right thing to say after all, for Malcolm sat up straighter, his usual stern countenance returning. "Sure, the family will make sure he gets the best care possible. But that doesn't excuse what he's done. . . . You know, I hate to admit this, but I really thought it was Lauren. I thought you were being fooled—because of your relationship with her. I even went to see her today. I thought maybe I could intimidate her, make her make a mistake. . . . God, I feel so stupid." Malcolm met Flynn's gaze and held it, his eyes grim. "He tried to destroy you, Flynn. That's hard enough to deal with. But using Uncle Bernard in this scheme! That I will never forgive." Malcolm stood slowly. "I'd better go back up there. There are people to call . . . arrangements to make."

Nodding, Flynn rose to his feet, facing him. "I'll see you at the office whenever you're ready. We have lots of work ahead of us."

That unspoken reassurance brought a small smile to Malcolm's thin lips, and when they shook hands, his grip lasted a bit longer than usual.

Flynn watched Malcolm's determined stride to the elevator. He knew the problems Chuck had caused were far from over—he'd have to face the press, the mayor, even his own staff, with some pretty harsh explanations. But his case against Blackford could be salvaged, and he'd make sure Malcolm got plenty of credit.

Right now, however, his most important concern was Lauren.

He waited until the elevator doors closed behind Malcolm before he made a dash for the gift shop. It was closed.

Stopping the first nurse he could find, he

explained, "I'm with the State Attorney's Office, and I need to see the night administrator."

Lauren woke to the mingled scents of flowers all around her. There were arrangements everywhere; a vase of tulips on the rolling table, containers of snapdragons, irises, and freesia on the windowsill, and on the bedside stand were two dozen fragrant long-stemmed red roses.

On the other side of her bed, Flynn was sprawled in a chair, sound asleep. He looked haggard. She wanted to run her fingers through his already tousled hair and kiss his stubbled chin until he smiled. But she couldn't move to reach him.

As if sensing her wakefulness, he suddenly opened his eyes. Gingerly, he joined her in the bed, carefully positioning himself so as not to disturb her bandaged arm. He pressed kisses on her eyelids, her brow, the tip of her nose, her cheeks, and finally, her lips.

While his fingers still played in her hair, he lifted his head and studied her face. She felt as fragile as fine porcelain. "How do you feel?" he asked her tenderly.

"I'm fine," she reassured him. "How did you get in here? . . . you look awful."

"I shamelessly used my clout as a public official. . . . You look beautiful," he whispered and proceeded to kiss her mouth thoroughly until they were both gasping for air.

"I can't even hug you," she wailed softly and he chuckled, resting his cheek on her breasts.

"That's all right. I'll do all the touching."

"I don't think they allow this in hospital rooms, Flynn," she warned softly, certain if she'd been hooked up to a pulse monitor a whole team of nurses would have rushed in to check on her.

Flynn nuzzled her through the thin hospital gown. "Tomorrow—no today, I'll bring you one of your silk nightgowns."

"Stop it! I'm totally helpless here."

"I know. I have you just where I want you. Remember in the hammock when I wouldn't let you go until I got the right answer from you?" He deposited another kiss at the corner of her mouth.

"Yes, of course, I remember. . . ."

"Well, again, I have you where I want you, so I'm going to take totally unfair advantage of you."

His face suddenly became uncharacteristically serious. He pushed himself up and took her chin between his gentle fingers.

"I think I was halfway in love with Dr. Jamieson's Lauren even before I met you. Now there's no halfway about it. . . . I love you."

His eyes had taken on an intent look

which she felt all the way to the pit of her stomach. Her pulse missed several beats, and the warmth in the lower part of her body spread everywhere. She swallowed once before trying to say anything.

"Flynn, I . . ."

He laid one finger over her lips, stopping her. "Lauren, I want every weekend to be like this last one. I want to wake up in the morning with your hair tickling my face. I want to sit in the evening dreaming into the fire with you by my side. I want to share everything with you. My life . . . my name . . . my love."

His urgency surprised and thrilled her at the same time. From Flynn she had not expected a plea. But she had dreamed about it, she now admitted freely. Dr. Jamieson's kindness and understanding had helped heal her wounds, but Flynn's love had made them fade to nothing.

She abandoned herself to the emotion she saw in his eyes, to the touch of his hands on her body.

For the first time, she looked at him with no shadows clouding her gaze. The blaze of love there shone forth, igniting a response in the fiery depths of Flynn's eyes.

"I'll gladly give you what you ask . . . all the years we have to love one another. . . . Just promise me one thing."

Flynn pulled back slightly. "Anything."

She arched an eyebrow at him. "Promise?"

"What is it that's so important?" he questioned, confused by her insistence.

"Right after the wedding, we exchange that hammock for a comfortable chaise longue."

Leslie Lynn is a pseudonym for sisters-in-law Sherrill Bodine and Elaine Sima, of Illinois. Avid readers, they have been collaborating on their writing for three years. *Buried Shadows* is their first novel.